COOS COOP

P9-CJC-360

3 2881 00799595 5

Conner turned and there was Tia, staring up at him with wide eyes. Was she going to get on his case too? Because it was the last thing he needed. "What?" he snapped.

Tia flinched. She grabbed onto her silver ring and began to twist it around and around her finger. "Nothing. I mean, I just wanted to talk."

"We already talked," Conner told Tia stiffly. He was starting to turn back around when Tia grabbed his arm. *Hard.*

Conner glanced at her and she let go.

"I *wanted* to talk about Angel," Tia said, her voice shaky and her big round eyes narrowing into slitted ovals. "About the fact that he has a new girlfriend and how much that hurts. I thought I could talk to my *best friend* about it. But I guess I was wrong." Tia glared at him for a moment longer, then stormed off, stalking right past Conner and into their homeroom.

You are such a jerk, McDermott.

Wonderful. Conner had only been awake for an hour and already this day sucked.

DISCARD

Don't miss any of the books in SWEET VALLEY HIGH
SENIOR YEAR, an exciting series from Bantam Books!

Visit the Official Sweet Valley Web Site on the Internet at:

http://www.sweetvalley.com

HAZEL M. LEWIS LIBRARY
POWERS, OREGON 97466

DATE DUE

BANTAM BOOKS
NEW YORK • TORONTO • LONDON • SYDNEY • AUCKLAND

RL: 6, AGES 012 AND UP

IT'S MY LIFE

A Bantam Book / July 2000

Sweet Valley High® is a registered trademark of Francine Pascal.
Conceived by Francine Pascal.
Cover photography by Michael Segal.

Copyright © 2000 by Francine Pascal.
Cover art copyright © 2000 by 17th Street Productions,
an Alloy Online, Inc. company.

All rights reserved. No part of this book may be reproduced or transmitted
in any form or by any means, electronic or mechanical, including
photocopying, recording, or by any information storage and retrieval
system, without permission in writing from the publisher.
For information address Bantam Books.

Produced by 17th Street Productions,
an Alloy Online, Inc. company.
33 West 17th Street
New York, NY 10011.

If you purchased this book without a cover you should be aware
that this book is stolen property. It was reported as "unsold and
destroyed" to the publisher and neither the author nor the publisher
has received any payment for this "stripped book."

ISBN: 0-553-49335-3

Visit us on the Web! www.randomhouse.com/teens

Published simultaneously in the United States and Canada

Bantam Books is an imprint of Random House Children's Books, a
division of Random House, Inc. BANTAM BOOKS and the rooster
colophon are registered trademarks of Random House, Inc. Bantam Books,
1540 Broadway, New York, New York 10036.

PRINTED IN THE UNITED STATES OF AMERICA

OPM   0 9 8 7 6 5 4 3 2 1

To Jamie Stewart

Ken Matthews

I didn't think it was possible for me to be more bummed out than I was at the beginning of the year. Well, Dad took care of that. He made it perfectly clear that he thinks I'm a loser. Thinks I'm nothing. A big, fat zero. A complete disappointment of his gene pool.

Maria says he's totally ridiculous. That he should be more proud of me than he's ever been in his life. I guess she's probably right.

But that doesn't exactly stop me from feeling like crap.

Jeremy Aames

Disappointments? Yeah, I've had my share of them. I've had <u>more</u> <u>than</u> my share of them. But do you want to know the pathetic thing? Even with all that stuff I went through when my father was sick and my family counted on me for everything, the disappointment that hit me the hardest was when Jessica dumped me.

Then again, at least I learned from that. I'll never let a girl disappoint me again.

TIA RAMIREZ

WHEN CONNER COMPLETELY
TORE INTO ME THE OTHER NIGHT,
I FELT ABOUT A MILLION THINGS
AT ONCE. HURT. ANGRY. WORRIED.
ANGRY. SAD. . . . DID I MENTION
ANGRY?

BUT ACTUALLY, THE MOST
OVERWHELMING EMOTION I FEEL
NOW IS DISAPPOINTMENT. NO,
NOT DISAPPOINTED THAT CONNER
AND I WILL NEVER BE INVOLVED.

DISAPPOINTED THAT MY BEST
FRIEND COULD ACTUALLY SAY
THOSE THINGS TO ME.

Andy Marsden

Funny. I've spent the past few days so disappointed in my friends for their unbelievable self-absorption that I haven't even let myself realize how I feel.

But since I've had some time now to sit with this, to think about it instead of talk about it, I'm actually okay about everything. Really. I'm gay, and I can deal with it.

. . . Um, I think.

CHAPTER
EMOTIONALLY DANGEROUS

1

The last thing Tia Ramirez wanted to do on Sunday morning was wake up. She knew that once she did, she'd be destined to spend the day exactly how she had occupied yesterday: hitting inanimate objects, crying, avoiding calls, moping, hiding in her room, and crying some more. She was definitely emotionally dangerous.

Tia groaned, digging her face deeper into her mass of down pillows and pulling her lacy white comforter more tightly around her body. Even if she wanted to wake up, it would be kind of hard, seeing as her eyelids were crusted shut from crying herself to sleep last night.

How could Conner be such a total jerk? Tia wondered for the umpteenth time as she tossed and turned in her bed. She wished she could just be mad at Conner. It would still suck, but at least it would make all of this easier. More straightforward. But after glimpsing that bottle of vodka in Conner's room on Friday night, Tia didn't know what to think—or feel. She wasn't sure if she should try to help Conner or kill him.

1

Her brain was a muddled mess. Her heart, a wreck.

Tia groaned again. Then, catching herself, she thought, *Wait a minute. What's wrong with me?* In a swift, sudden movement Tia opened her eyes and sat up straight, throwing her covers off. *This is so totally pathetic,* she realized as she glanced around her room and noticed all of the wadded-up tissues scattered across her floor.

"Okay. You have to get a grip," Tia mumbled, disgusted with herself. She hopped out of bed and began to collect the Kleenex debris. This was so unlike her. She was not the type to wallow. She *hated* when people wallowed.

Shaking her head, Tia dumped the tissues in her trash basket under her desk. Then she marched into her bathroom to throw some cold water on her face. She cringed when she saw her reflection in the mirror above her sink. Her large brown eyes were rimmed with red, and her skin was all blotchy.

"Pathetic," Tia muttered. She grabbed a red scrunchie off a shelf and pulled her long, brown hair into a ponytail. Then she turned on the faucet and scrubbed her face with a vengeance. Maybe if she scrubbed hard enough, she could get rid of all the hurt.

Okay, she thought when she was finished. She took a deep breath as she dried her face with a towel. *You just need to clear your head. Figure this all out.*

Then again, that's what she'd tried to do yesterday. And look where it had gotten her. A state of total brain mush.

No, she realized as she stepped back into her room. She'd have to talk this through with someone. Someone stable. Someone who could help her make sense of everything.

Angel. His name immediately popped into Tia's head. She bit her lip at the thought. All right, so she hadn't really spoken to him since they had broken up. But Angel was the definition of stability. Of rational thought. Besides, Angel had been Tia's sounding board for years. He would understand why she needed him right now. He'd have to.

Without a second thought, Tia grabbed the cordless phone off her desk and dialed Angel's number. As the phone rang on the other end, Tia slowly walked toward her bed, fidgeting with the drawstring on her pajama bottoms with her free hand.

"Hello?"

At the sound of Angel's voice unexpected tears instantly sprang to Tia's eyes. And they weren't I-want-you-back tears. They were the kind of tears she got when she was really sad and she spoke to someone superclose to her, like her mom. The uncontrollable kind of tears.

Tia dropped down onto her bed, feeling like the wind had been knocked out of her. God, she was such a disaster.

"Hi, Angel," Tia said, trying hard to keep the pain out of her voice. She winced at how weak she sounded.

"Tia?" Angel responded, surprise evident in his tone. "Hey . . . are you okay?"

Tia sat back against her pillows, pulling her knees up to her chest and closing her eyes. *Keep it together,* she recited to herself.

But hearing Angel sound so concerned only made it worse. Now the tears began to roll down her cheeks. Tia tasted salt as one tear made it to her mouth.

"Um, no," Tia sniffled. "I guess—I guess I'm not." She rubbed her nose with the back of her hand as her breathing began to come out in shallow gasps. *Lovely, Tee,* she thought. Still, now that she had him on the phone, there was no point in trying to hide her crying. This was Angel. He'd be able to tell anyway.

"I just really need you," Tia went on, trying to find her voice. "I mean, I need . . . I need to talk to you."

"You do?" Angel sounded weird. Strained, almost.

Tia grabbed a tissue from the box on her bedside table and blew into it. At some point she was going to have to start making sense.

"Yeah," she responded, nodding even though no one could see her. "All this stuff has been going on, Angel, and you're the—"

"Wait a sec," Angel broke in. "Listen, before you go on, there's something you should know."

Tia crumpled the tissue. Her dark eyebrows scrunched together. "Huh? What do you mean?"

"I've missed you too," Angel told her gently. "And I've wanted you back—us back—at times also."

Tia's eyes widened, and her grip on the tissue tightened. *Oh my God*. He thought that she wanted—

"Wait, Angel, this isn't—"

"Just let me finish," he interrupted. "Let me get this out. I mean, I wanted to tell you anyway."

Tia's head was spinning. She clasped onto the edge of her pillow, tissue still in hand. Could it be? Did Angel want to get back together? "Tell me what?"

There was a brief, impossibly heavy pause and then: "I'm seeing someone."

The words cut like glass. Tia grasped the phone tighter. She started to sweat. Her head pounded. And her heart began to beat at a crazy, deafening rate.

There was only one logical thing that Tia could do now. So she did it.

She hung up.

Jade Wu woke up late on Sunday morning. Still lying underneath her blue-and-pink patchwork quilt, she regarded her Hello Kitty alarm clock with one open eye. Eleven-fifteen. Actually, compared to Jade's normal weekend wake-up time of 2 P.M., it was on the early side.

Jade sat up and yawned, pushing her tangled hair away from her face. *Hey. Mom could even still be home*, she realized. After all, it was before noon.

Jade yawned again, then stood and slid her feet into her fuzzy Winnie-the-Pooh slippers. She grabbed her red-and-black kimono bathrobe up off her clothes-covered floor and pulled it on over her baby-doll nightie.

Her eyes half closed, Jade padded out into the hallway. Her mother's bedroom door, which was directly across from Jade's, was wide open. Jade peered inside. There was no movement. No sound. No sign of her mom.

Jade stood there for a moment, staring at her mother's empty, unmade queen-size bed, the light gray sheets blowing a little from the breeze that was coming through the window her mother had left open.

Probably out with the new guy of the week—Mike . . . or was it Mark? Not that Jade cared or anything. She was used to this. Which was why she was such an expert at being alone. But for some reason, right now she felt like having a little company.

Jade turned around, heading for her narrow kitchen at the end of the hall. *Because last night was so boring,* she reminded herself as she opened the refrigerator and pulled out a two-liter bottle of Dr Pepper. Jade hadn't been able to get together any exciting plans the night before, so she'd ended up spending the whole long evening camped out on her couch in front of the TV. Boring was an understatement.

Jade was just pouring some soda into a mug when the phone rang. The sound was a welcome break in the silence of the house. Mug in hand, Jade stepped into the living room and grabbed the cordless. "Hello?"

"Jade?"

Jade smiled. She could tell by the hint of nervousness in the guy's voice that it was Jeremy. She dropped down on the couch's armrest. "Hi, Jeremy."

"Hey. I didn't wake you, did I?" he asked.

"Almost." Jade crossed her legs, swinging them in front of her. "I got up a couple of minutes ago."

"Have a good night last night?"

Jade contemplated her mug of Dr Pepper. "Mildly entertaining." Jade didn't mean to lie, but she knew it wasn't in her best interests to tell a guy that she'd had no plans. It was one of the most basic rules. You had to keep them guessing to keep them interested.

"Sounds better than my night," Jeremy commented. "I did nothing. I was parked in front of the TV."

Jade smiled again. Of course, it didn't hurt to know that *he* had been home alone all evening. "Poor baby," she teased.

"I know." Jeremy laughed. "Anyway, I can't really talk. I promised my sisters I'd take them to the movies."

Jade took a long sip of her soda, playfully rolling her eyes. Jeremy was such the model older brother. He was the model *everything*.

"I just called to say hi," he went on. "And to see if you wanted to go out again. Uh, with me. Tomorrow night."

Jade's dark eyes lit up at both the cute way Jeremy sputtered out the suggestion and at the thought of another date. She laughed, standing up. "Sure. That'd be fun."

7

"Yeah? Cool. Well, gotta go. I'll call you tomorrow, okay?"

Cradling the phone between her neck and shoulder, Jade twirled a strand of her long hair around her finger. "Yeah. Okay."

"Good. Well, bye. Oh—and Jade?"

She raised her eyebrows. "Yes?"

"Have a great day."

Jeremy hung up, and Jade bit her lip, trying to prevent a supremely goofy smile from spreading across her face. She hit the talk button on the phone, then tossed it back onto the couch.

At least there are major bonuses to Mom never being home, she thought, tapping her lilac-painted fingernail against the now empty mug. *Like never having to ask for permission.*

And with that energizing thought, Jade ran into her room to blast the stereo.

Tia felt rather numb as she rang Andy Marsden's doorbell a couple of hours later. There were so many thoughts and emotions battling themselves out in her brain that she couldn't process any of them. The only thing Tia *did* know was that she was upset. Catastrophically upset. Come to think of it, *upset* probably wasn't even the word to describe it.

Tia wrapped her old gray hooded sweatshirt close to her body, hugging herself. It was an overcast, windy day. More than fitting for Tia's mood.

With the way my luck's been going, Andy's proba-bly not even home, she thought, kicking at the Marsdens' ratty woven doormat. But just as Tia let out a big frustrated sigh, the door opened and Andy stood before her.

Andy's blue eyes opened wide the second he saw her. "Hey," he said. "Tee? What's wrong?"

Perfect. I must look like a freak or something. Tia glanced down at the doormat, then looked back up at Andy. She managed a half smile. "Um, everything?"

"All righty, then." Andy grabbed her tiny arm, pulling her inside. "Looks like you need to talk."

Tia silently followed Andy up the Marsdens' car-peted staircase, grateful that he was always there for her. Suddenly she didn't know what she would do without him.

"So. What's up?" Andy asked as they reached his bedroom. He closed the door behind them.

Tia trudged over and plopped onto Andy's gray platform bed. Leaning against the wall, she grabbed his plaid pillow and hugged it, bringing her knees up to her chest. This was a familiar position for Tia. Pretty much the one she'd been in for the past two days.

"Let's see. Where do I begin?" She picked at a loose thread on the pillowcase as she spoke. "Oh, right. Well, I spoke to Angel today, and he has a new girlfriend." The thread slipped from Tia's fingers. Just saying the words made her stomach turn.

"Whoa. Wow, Tee. That's . . . heavy." Andy moved

his rolling desk chair closer to the bed and turned it around, dropping down into it and straddling it backward. He didn't say anything more for a couple of moments.

Tia stared at him, wide-eyed. Was that it? Was that all he was going to say? *Heavy?* That wasn't exactly the most helpful advice. Actually, it wasn't even *advice*.

Andy leaned forward, resting his arms on the back of the seat. "So, uh, who is she?"

Tia's shoulders collapsed. She let go of the pillow and rolled her eyes. "How do I know? I didn't *ask*."

Andy looked confused. "You didn't?"

Tia sighed. "No. I hung up on him," she stated, as if it should've been perfectly obvious that's what she would've done. Which, in Tia's mind, it should have been.

Now Andy looked even more confused. He scratched his head. "Oh."

This was pointless. Tia stood up. She didn't want to talk about Angel anymore. Besides, he wasn't the source of her real problems. Or at least he shouldn't be.

Tia gently kicked at a pile of dirty clothes on the floor by Andy's bed. "Angel's not even why I'm upset anyway," she muttered.

"Uh-huh," Andy responded, his tone reflecting his lack of belief in her statement.

Tia glanced up at Andy midkick. God, why did she even mention the Angel thing? "Really." She dropped her foot to the floor and stared Andy down, placing her hands on her hips. "I'm serious, Andy. What's really bothering me is that Conner's been drinking lately, okay?"

Confusion, Andy's apparent emotion of the day, once again presented itself on his features. "Conner's drinking? That's not exactly a news flash."

"Yeah. I know." Tia pushed a strand of her dark hair away from her face. "But what I'm talking about is different. I mean, he's been acting really weird."

An ambulance siren blared from outside. Andy sat up straight, as if he was jolted from the sound. "Weird how?"

The sound of the siren moved into the distance. But that didn't stop Tia's head from pounding. "I don't know. . . . Just . . . weird," she insisted. How could she possibly explain this? Andy knew Tia and Conner had kissed, and he knew she'd been wondering if maybe something more could happen between them. So if she admitted the way Conner had rejected her so harshly the other night, it would seem like she was just disappointed that Conner wasn't interested or something. But that really wasn't it.

Tia walked over to Andy's desk, picking up a chewed-up pencil and fidgeting with it as she tried to figure out how to phrase this.

"*Oo*-kay," Andy commented.

Tia took a deep breath. She focused on the teeth-marked orange-yellow Mongol no. 2 between her fingers. "Fine. Like, the other night, I went over to Conner's. He was alone, and—" Tia bit her lip, abruptly cutting herself off. She couldn't bear to tell Andy the rest. To repeat the words that Conner had used against her. It hurt enough just thinking about it.

So she just glanced up at Andy, speechless.

He had swiveled the chair around to face her. "And what?" he pressed.

Tia sighed. She shook her head. "And nothing." She put down the pencil and pulled herself onto the desk, her short legs dangling in the air. "You know what? I don't even know why I'm so upset," she lied. "I'm probably just overreacting."

Andy stood, running a hand through his red hair. "Yeah. Sounds like it."

"Yeah." *That got me absolutely nowhere,* Tia thought miserably.

The two friends were quiet for a moment. Tia stared down at her sneakers, her mind still reeling, as Andy walked over to the window and stared outside.

So much for talking this through with someone.

"Um, Tee?" Andy said suddenly, sharply cutting the thick silence and pulling Tia out of her thoughts.

She glanced up. "Yeah?"

Andy turned away from the window, facing Tia. He stuck his hands in his jeans' back pockets. His eyes darted to the ceiling, then fell back down to Tia. "Uh, this probably isn't the best time to mention this or anything, but I want you to hear it from me, not

12

Jessica or Maria or Liz—and I talked to them about it last night at HOJ."

Tia grasped onto the edge of the desk. Perfect. What now? "Okay," she said warily.

Andy closed his eyes, then opened them again. He tugged at the ripped neckline of his purple T-shirt. "Well, it's just that I think I'm . . . gay."

Tia blinked. "You think you're *what?*"

Andy stared down at the carpeting, color rising in his cheeks. "Gay," he mumbled. "I think that I might be gay."

For a long moment Tia simply stared at her friend, trying to digest this information. Actually, the idea had occurred to Tia many times, and she'd always sort of suspected it. But the fact that *Andy* had realized it himself and that he was telling her . . . *and Jess and Maria and Liz* . . . this was big. *This* was heavy.

"Wow," she said finally, sliding off the desk. "How long have you, uh, known?"

Andy scratched the back of his neck, shifting his weight from one foot to the other. "It's not really like I *know*. I'm just sort of working this all out, I guess."

Biting her lip, Tia walked over and gave Andy a big hug. She was relieved when he squeezed her back tightly. At least he knew she was there for him.

"Well, congratulations," Tia said, still holding on to him. "I mean, on starting to figure stuff out, at least. Or whatever." She tried not to wince at her clumsy language.

13

Then she pulled away and looked at Andy's face. His rather *anxious* face.

"Uh, thanks," he mumbled, taking a step back.

Man. Poor guy. Suddenly Tia felt like the worst friend on the planet. Here she had been babbling about her inconsequential problems while Andy was struggling with major issues of sexual orientation. Could she possibly be any more selfish?

Tia reached out and laid her hand on his arm. "So you haven't told anyone else yet?" she asked. "Besides Liz, Maria, and Jessica?"

Andy shook his head, still fidgeting with the bottom of his shirt. "It's not exactly something you go door-to-door with," he said with a small shrug. "I'm not even sure what to say."

So he hasn't talked to Conner about it, Tia found herself noting. This was ridiculous—couldn't she forget about Conner McDermott for two seconds, especially when Andy obviously needed her?

"Let's go to House of Java," Tia suggested. "We'll grab some coffee and talk. You can totally unload on me. And I promise, no more discussion about my idiotic concerns."

Andy squinted, seeming to consider it for a brief moment. Then he shook his head. "Thanks," he said. "But I'm actually kinda okay about this. Right now, at least. And you seem a little crazed. I'll take a rain check."

"No way." Tia put her hands on her hips, regarding

her friend with wide eyes. "I'm not *that* crazed. And I *want* to talk about this."

"We will," Andy assured her. "Just later. I don't even have that much to say about it right now."

Tia arched an eyebrow. "You sure?"

Andy smiled. "Positive."

Tia pulled Andy into another hug. "Okay," she told him. "But I'm here whenever you need me."

And she meant it.

After all, Andy was the one guy in her life who *hadn't* let her down.

Megan Sandborn

I've decided that Conner is determined <u>never</u> to be happy. Everything's finally good at home— Mom's back <u>and</u> sober, and Conner and Liz are finally together like they should be. My brother should be ecstatic. Thrilled. But is he? Of course not.

Lately he's acting even more grumpy than usual. And given all the good things going on in his life, I just can't figure out what his deal is. I mean, the other day he almost completely lost it on me for no reason. And as annoyed as Conner always gets at everyone else, he usually never gets angry at <u>me.</u>

But then, just when I was ready to avoid him at all costs, Conner came home tonight all psyched. He couldn't stop talking about this gig he scored at The Shack—a place in Palisades.

Hey. Maybe that's it. Maybe this past week Conner's just been tense about his music and about auditioning for this manager. Yeah. That has to be what's been going on. And now that Conner got the gig, he should be back to normal.

Um . . . as normal as Conner ever is.

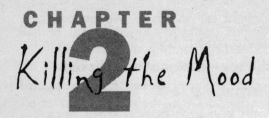

CHAPTER 2
Killing the Mood

Maybe he'll be sick, Tia thought as she navigated her way down the crowded hallway toward homeroom on Monday morning. *Maybe he got so trashed last night that he didn't wake up for school.*

Of course Tia didn't actually *want* Conner to be passed out drunk, but at the moment that almost seemed better than having to deal with him today.

I'll just ignore him, Tia decided, making her way around a large group of freshman girls annoyingly stopped right in the middle of the hall. *No, no, I'll yell at him . . . or maybe I'll talk to him, but—*

"Hey, Tee."

Tia stopped dead in her tracks. She'd been so busy plotting what she would do when she saw Conner that she didn't actually *see* him walking toward her from the other direction. And now here he was, standing right in front of her.

And looking kind of normal. Smiling, almost. Or smiling in the Conner definition of a smile, with half of his mouth drawn up. His green eyes actually seemed alive. Happy.

Had Conner completely forgotten that he had basically killed their friendship the other night?

"So, uh, I've got some good news," he said.

Tia blinked. Apparently he had. Had she dreamed the whole episode? Or maybe this was part of his apology? She crossed her arms over her chest. "Yeah?"

Conner stuck his left hand in the front pocket of his trademark old Levi's. "Evan's friend Mike Legum knows this guy who runs a club in Palisades. I met the guy yesterday, played for him a little, and scored a gig for this weekend."

A wayward backpack suddenly smacked Tia from behind, and she stumbled forward. "Hey, watch it!" she yelled at no one in particular. Then she sighed and focused back on Conner.

Okay, so if she'd processed this correctly, he had a gig. Now there he went with that little half smile of his. Tia didn't get it. Was she supposed to be happy for him? Actually, despite everything, she kind of was— almost like a reflex response. But she wasn't about to give Conner the satisfaction of letting him know that.

"Cool," she said distantly. One-syllable words were about all she could muster right now. Otherwise she'd just lose it. And she didn't have the energy for that at the moment.

"Yeah." Conner shifted his black backpack from his right shoulder to his left. "The place is much bigger than HOJ. And people go there to hear music. Not to, you know, drink coffee."

Tia stared blankly at him for a moment longer. Then came the eruption. "Conner?" she snapped, her face heating up as the anger built inside her at a multiplying rate. "Are you going to say *anything* about Friday night? Or am I supposed to just pretend it never happened?"

Conner raised his eyebrows. Then he looked down at the floor. "Uh, sorry about that." He glanced back at Tia and ran a hand through his scruffy hair. "You just caught me at a bad time, Tee. I was really wound up."

The first bell rang as Tia's brain reeled. *You caught me at a bad time?* Tia silently repeated, clenching her teeth. *That* was Conner's excuse for treating her like total trash? One day he was kissing her and the next he was dumping all over her, and Tia was supposed to accept the lame explanation that he was simply in a bad mood? "Uh-huh," was all Tia could say, all the while leveling Conner with a glare.

"Anyway." Conner motioned to their homeroom door with his eyes. "Wanna go in?"

Tia sighed. The truly pathetic aspect of this whole situation was that she knew that in Conner speak, that bit of mumbling he'd just come out with translated into a heartfelt apology. But still, that didn't mean Tia had to forgive him.

Tia looked at the ground, chewing on the inside of her lip. Then again, what were her options? Forget about ten years of friendship and just be mad at

Conner forever? Eventually she'd have to get past this, and Conner probably wasn't going to make much more of an effort than he was right now. She glanced back up at him. He was awkwardly shifting the weight of his backpack from one shoulder to the other again. Well . . . she was definitely still angry. There was no way to change that. But maybe, just maybe, she could give the guy a chance to make it up to her. If that was even possible.

Tia nodded slightly. "Yeah. Okay," she muttered. It was all she could handle at this point.

As Tia followed Conner toward the door, part of her clung to the hope that Andy had been right last night. Maybe she had been overreacting. Maybe there was really no reason to worry about Conner at all.

Tia grasped onto the strap of her backpack. Unfortunately, somehow the rest of her couldn't quite believe it.

Something was seriously wrong with this picture. At the moment Elizabeth Wakefield was sitting behind Conner on his iron-frame bed, with both her legs and arms wrapped around him, covering the back of his neck with a trail of tingling kisses.

But unfortunately, although his body might be responding to Elizabeth's kisses—goose bumps were making their way from the bottom of his hairline down his back—Conner's brain was somewhere else entirely.

You have to do better on Friday, he told himself,

staring down at his guitar, which he had just placed on the bed next to him after playing his newest song for Elizabeth. *Much better.*

"That was incredible, Conner," Elizabeth whispered between kisses. "You're going to be so great."

A glimmer of hope revived him. Conner turned his head, glancing at Elizabeth sideways. "You think so?"

She turned Conner all the way around so that he was facing her. Her aqua eyes were bright. She nodded, and her silky blond hair fell in front of her face. "Definitely. No doubt."

For a split second Conner gazed back at Elizabeth, and he actually believed her. *Liz liked the song. So maybe—*

But that moment disappeared fast. *She's your girlfriend, idiot. She's in love with you. Of course she's going to tell you you're good.*

Still, Conner leaned in and kissed Elizabeth as a thank-you. It wasn't her fault that she was going out with a talentless idiot who had delusions about being a rock star.

Elizabeth let out a small sigh, and Conner moved his kisses over to her shoulder. He slid down the neckline of her cotton scoop-neck sweater and put his lips to the smooth, bare skin where her shoulder rounded, closing his eyes and taking in the light floral scent of her perfume.

Conner wished he could forget everything and lose himself in Elizabeth. But one thought kept running through his brain: *You're going to suck, McDermott. You're going to suck, and that'll be it.*

It sort of killed the mood for him.

Frustrated, Conner drew Elizabeth's sweater back up and pulled away. But Elizabeth didn't sense his anxiety. Or if she did, she pretended not to. Smiling, she cupped his chin with her hand and gave him one last, lingering kiss. Then she broke away and glanced at her watch.

"Shoot. I gotta go," Elizabeth told him, her full lips turning down into a frown. She reached to grab her brown leather backpack off the floor, then hesitated, regarding Conner playfully for a second. She traced the neckline of his worn-out T-shirt with her finger. "Do you promise you'll remember me when you're rich and famous?"

Conner scratched his head, pretending to give the matter extensive thought. But deep down, he knew it wasn't an issue. There was no way he would ever be even close to famous. "I'll try."

Elizabeth whacked him on the shoulder. "Gee, thanks," she said with a laugh. She stood up and shrugged her backpack onto her shoulders, then kissed the top of Conner's head. "Call me later?"

Conner nodded, feeling dejected. "Yeah."

"All right. Bye," Elizabeth said. And then she walked out.

Conner sat on his bed, staring at his closed bedroom door. He knew he needed to practice some more, but he couldn't deal with facing the frustration of playing badly. Still, what was he going to do? Not practice and bomb out in front of all those people? Sighing, Conner turned and reached for his guitar and began to play.

He sounded horrible. Like a total amateur.

Conner threw the guitar back down on the bed. *Crap*. He had to do better. He had to *nail* this song. The Shack was a big place. Much bigger than HOJ. And it attracted a totally different crowd. A whole new audience.

Conner stood, grasping at his hair, wanting to pull it all out. He stalked over to his window and then over to his desk, unable to stay in one place in his narrow room. He walked back over to the window again, fidgeting with the plastic wand attached to his blinds.

Conner knew that if he wasn't so tense and frustrated, he'd probably be okay. He always played better when he was relaxed. But the thing was, he *was* tense and he *was* frustrated. He couldn't exactly just make all that disappear.

Or maybe he could . . .

Conner glanced over at his closet, where he had hidden that bottle of vodka he'd bought a few days ago from Bob's Spirits, a seedy liquor store that was famous for not caring if you were of age or not. Conner had spotted the store on his way back from talking to the manager at The Shack and had figured, why not? *Might as well pick up something just in case.* There were always times when you just needed it.

And this is definitely one of those times, Conner decided. He walked over to his closet and dug out the tall, clear glass bottle, which was buried underneath his socks and underwear. He'd only take a sip or two. Just enough to relax.

Conner unscrewed the cap and took a swig. At first he winced from the harshness of the alcohol, but soon he felt the liquid travel slowly down his body, settling in his stomach and emanating waves of warmth. Conner sat down on his bed and closed his eyes. He already felt better. Looser. One more swig and he'd be there.

Conner took a second gulp. Yeah. This was exactly what he needed. He placed the bottle down on his unstained wooden floor and picked his guitar back up. After strumming out a few chords, relief surged through him. Now, *that* was more like it.

Conner's eyes fell back down to the bottle of vodka. He stopped playing for a moment as he considered it. One more swig couldn't hurt, right? Just to take the edge off.

Reaching for the bottle, he took another sip. And he smiled.

There. Now he was just about perfect.

* * *

Jeremy Aames mentally patted himself on the back for creating such an incredible evening.

What, exactly, was so incredible about it?

Let's see . . . at the moment Jade Wu, one of the cutest girls Jeremy had ever laid eyes on, was leaning back into him, cuddled into his arms. Jeremy was glad that Jade was sitting *in front* of him, because if she saw the lame smile on his face, she would definitely call for the dork squad. Jeremy also didn't mind staring down at Jade's head of beautiful thick, glossy black hair. The honey-tinged scent of her shampoo was driving him crazy.

Not to mention that Jade and Jeremy were presently sitting at one of Jeremy's favorite places in the world—the huge, flat cliff in Hyde Park, one of the highest points in El Carro. Jeremy smiled to himself, running a hand through his brown hair. He had timed this all so perfectly. He and Jade now had the pleasure of watching the setting sun plunge downward, back lighting the tissuelike clouds with brilliant pinks and oranges.

Jade seemed to be enjoying taking it all in. "I bet you lure all the girls up here," she commented, twirling a strand of hair around her finger.

Jeremy craned his head around to try to glance down at her face. He could never tell when Jade was serious. But at the moment she didn't seem to be smiling. Did she really think he was some kind of player? What a joke.

"Not exactly," Jeremy told her, resting his chin on the top of her head. "Actually, my dad used to take me here a lot when I was little."

Jade pulled away, turning around to look at him. Her black eyes danced with amusement. "Aw. How sweet," she teased, lightly poking his chest.

Jeremy felt his cheeks flame up. *You have to stop saying things like that.* Jade already thought he was a total goody-goody as it was. Going on about his Brady Bunch family memories wasn't going to help matters.

"Well, I like it here," Jade added, standing up and surveying the 360-degree scene spread out before them. "It's really cool."

Jeremy relaxed. So she approved. That was good. Very good. "Yeah. I think so too." He zipped up his thin blue jacket to combat the chilly wind.

Jade's mouth formed into a slow smile, her long, straight hair flying around her face. Her arms disappeared inside the sleeves of her oversized black rollnecked sweater as she hugged herself to keep warm. The girl was definitely gorgeous. No question about that.

Then Jade turned and skipped toward the edge of the cliff. *Uncomfortably close* to the edge.

Gorgeous and nuts, Jeremy added silently, standing up. He was about to call out to her to move back but caught himself. That wouldn't exactly help him get rid of his squeaky-clean image, now, would it?

HAZEL M. LEWIS LIBRARY
POWERS, OREGON 97466

Still, Jeremy felt uneasy as he watched Jade stand there with her back to him, reaching her arms out on either side of her and grasping at the wind. She looked impossibly tiny in her huge sweater and black pants, her small frame set against the backdrop of the seemingly endless hills, valleys, and, in the far distance, mountains.

Finally Jade turned around. She took a few steps away from the edge and walked back toward Jeremy. He let out a little breath of relief.

"So . . . where *do* you usually take girls?" Jade asked playfully, sitting down next to where Jeremy was standing. She pulled her sweater over her knees, curling her body into a ball.

Jeremy laughed. He sat as well, watching her with questioning eyes. "What makes you think there've been so many girls?"

Jade shrugged. She rested her cheek between her knees so that she was looking at Jeremy sideways. "Just wondering." Then she lifted her head, raising an eyebrow, as if a thought had just popped into her head. "Hey. Have you ever been in love?"

Oh, man. Do we have to talk about this? Jeremy felt his stomach sink into his New Balance sneakers. His immediate, instinctual answer was *yes*. Yes, he'd been in love with Jessica Wakefield. But then again, he hadn't gone out with all that many girls. Maybe it hadn't been love. Maybe it was just very strong like. Besides, Jeremy and Jessica's relationship had died such a pathetic death. How could it have been love?

"Jeremy?" Jade prompted. "Are you with me?"

Jeremy glanced at her, then looked down at his shoes, fidgeting with his laces as his earlobes started to burn. Either way, telling a girl on your second date that you'd been in love with someone else wasn't exactly romantic, was it?

Jeremy hesitated a moment more as he tried to figure out the best way to respond without lying altogether. "Well . . . I think I may have been," he managed finally, looking back at Jade. "But I guess I'm not sure."

"Ah." Jade shook her head knowingly. "Then you haven't. You'd *know*."

Jeremy's eyes clouded over. In that case, he *had* most definitely been in love with Jessica. Without a doubt. He'd known it from the beginning. *No wonder she was so hard to get over,* Jeremy thought, annoyed, wrapping his shoelace so tightly around his finger that he almost cut off his circulation.

"Jeremy?" Jade's eyes squinted into narrow slits. "What are you thinking about?"

"Huh?" He shook his head, as if to banish all thoughts of Jessica from his brain. The important thing was, Jeremy *had* gotten over her. And now he was here with Jade. A beautiful, fun, cool girl. Who he didn't want to mess things up with. "Nothing," he stated, forcing a smile. "Nothing at all."

Jade chewed on the inside of her lip, nodding slowly. "Whatever you say."

Clearly Jade didn't believe him. And she could obviously tell that he'd been flustered there for a moment. Well, Jeremy wasn't going to let Jessica mess up this perfect evening with Jade. He had to convince Jade that she was the only girl on his mind.

So he grabbed both of her hands, pulling her toward him. And he kissed her.

Jeremy couldn't tell if Jade was convinced. But he sure was.

TIA RAMIREZ

REASONS WHY I SHOULD STILL BE MAD AT CONNER

- THAT APOLOGY WAS SERIOUSLY PATHETIC.
- HE HAS TO LEARN THAT HE CAN'T GET AWAY WITH THINGS LIKE THIS. "THAT'S JUST HOW CONNER IS" DOESN'T CUT IT ANYMORE.
- WHAT HE SAID REALLY HURT ME. A LOT.

REASONS WHY I SHOULD ACCEPT CONNER'S APOLOGY

- WE'VE BEEN FRIENDS FOREVER.
- HE DID ACTUALLY USE THE WORDS I'M SORRY. THAT'S A FIRST.
- WHAT AM I GOING TO DO? STAY MAD AT HIM FOREVER?
- BESIDES, WHAT WOULD I DO WITHOUT HIM?

CHAPTER 3
A Freakin' Mind Reader

When Conner woke up on Tuesday morning, his mouth felt drier than the Arizona desert.

Water, he thought, lifting his head from his guitar, which he'd apparently used as a pillow last night. *Need water.* Conner slowly sat up and dropped his feet to the floor, his limbs feeling unusually heavy and achy. He brought a hand to the back of his neck, trying to rub out the stiffness. *Man.* His head was *pounding.*

Conner glimpsed the half-empty bottle of vodka sitting on the floor by his bed, then glanced away. He tried to remember when he had fallen asleep, but he had no clue. Looking down at himself, Conner realized that he'd slept in the clothes he'd been wearing last night.

Who cares, he thought, pulling himself up and trudging out into the hall. *Just get some water.* He walked into the bathroom and turned on the faucet in the sink, cupping his hands to catch the dripping lukewarm water and slurping it down as fast as possible.

When he was done, he reached to open the medicine cabinet to grab some aspirin. Conner hesitated as he caught his reflection in the cabinet's mirror. Lines from the guitar strings were imbedded in the left side of his face. His green eyes were red and bloodshot. And his short hair was sticking out in all directions.

"Whatever," he mumbled, pulling out a bottle of Tylenol. He swallowed three pills, figuring he could use the extra strength. Anything to get rid of this headache. Then Conner quickly brushed his teeth, splashed some water on his face, and sprayed on some Right Guard. Ready to go.

As Conner opened the bathroom door, his half sister, Megan, who was headed for the stairs at Mach speed, whipped her head around. "Conner! You're late!" she exclaimed.

Conner winced at the shrill sound of her voice. "Don't worry about it," he muttered, walking into his room and slamming the door behind him. *Oops. Ouch. That was loud.*

He glanced at the digital clock by his bed. He *was* late. *Must've hit the snooze button a few times.* Of course, he didn't even remember hearing the alarm go off.

Well, it didn't matter. It wouldn't take Conner long to get ready. He simply took off his white T-shirt from the night before and pulled on a semi-clean gray one, stuck his feet into his work boots, grabbed his backpack, and hid the bottle of vodka back in the closet, and he was out of there.

I'll grab some cold water and I'll be golden, he thought as he made his way down the stairs.

When Conner trudged into the kitchen, his mother was perched on one of the tall wooden stools by the Formica counter, reading *USA Today* as she sipped her coffee. *All right,* Conner thought as he glimpsed her. The key here was to just get the water and then make a quick exit.

"Morning," Conner grunted, heading straight for the refrigerator.

"Morning, honey," his mom said from behind him. "You're running a little late, aren't you? Megan already left with her friends."

Conner rolled his eyes as he gulped some Poland Spring. You'd think the world was going to fall apart if he was fifteen minutes late for school. He put the cap back on the plastic water bottle and closed the refrigerator.

"I'll get there in time," he said, turning around.

Conner's mother's light eyebrows scrunched together the second she looked at him. She lifted up her reading glasses, placing them on top of her mass of dyed blond hair, and stared at Conner with worried-looking eyes.

"Conner? Are you feeling all right?" She slid off the stool and walked over to him, putting a hand to his forehead.

Conner took a step back, moving her hand away. This mother routine of hers really was amusing. Unfortunately, Conner wasn't in the mood this morning to see the humor in it. "Yes," he told her. "I was just up late practicing."

"I don't know," Mrs. Sandborn said, crossing her arms over her chest and staring at Conner's face. "You look awful. Maybe you should stay home."

Ah. Words of parental advice from the woman who'd been passed out drunk for the past five years. How meaningful. Too bad Conner didn't need to be told what to do.

"I can take care of myself, thanks," he snapped. Then he turned and stormed toward the front door.

Unbelievable. Conner actually *wanted* to go to school today.

At least no one would bother him there.

"Did you oversleep too?"

Conner shut the door of his black Mustang convertible twenty minutes later and turned around to see Maria Slater hurrying toward him, her silver bracelets jangling as she ran. He rolled his eyes. He wasn't in the mood for mindless chitchat. "I guess," Conner mumbled, starting to walk.

Maria rushed to catch up to him. "My stupid alarm must be broken," she ranted, breathless, as she tossed her car keys into the small front section of her backpack. She zipped it up and then shrugged the bag onto her shoulders. "I almost didn't find a parking space."

How tragic, Conner thought, silently continuing toward the school steps. Why was Maria so stressed out? There were still plenty of people hanging out on the stairs, which meant that the first bell hadn't even rung yet. And even if it had, who cared?

Maria touched Conner's arm. He glanced at her, annoyed. *What now?*

"You okay, Conner?" she asked, searching his face, her dark eyes wide with concern. "You don't look so hot."

Perfect. She was going to play mother too? "I'm fine," he grunted as they began to climb the stairs.

"*Oo*-kay," Maria responded sarcastically.

Conner gripped onto both straps of his backpack, needing to let the tension out on something. He briefly closed his eyes as they reached the school entrance. *Just relax,* he told himself. *Get away from Miss Chipper, and you'll be okay.*

He opened his eyes and walked inside. Breaking away from Maria turned out not to be all that difficult since she quickly disappeared down the hall without so much as a second word to Conner. *Good. She got the point.*

Conner let out a sigh. The morning bustle of students was a little much for him today. He trudged along slowly, trying to dodge the crowds.

"Hey, McD!"

Conner glanced ahead and saw that Evan Plummer and Andy were hanging out by their lockers.

"Whoa. Looking a little pale," Andy remarked as Conner headed toward them.

"Yeah. You feelin' all right?" Evan put in, grabbing a physics textbook out of his locker.

Man. What was with everybody today? Was there a reason they all found it necessary to remark on his appearance? "I'm fine," Conner snapped. "You know, you guys look like crap too."

Conner saw Andy and Evan exchange a look conveying *what the hell?*, but Conner didn't care. His head was still throbbing, his body was aching, and he was now breaking out into a clammy sweat. He didn't need Andy and Evan's lame observations on top of it.

The first bell rang. "Later," he muttered to them, heading in the direction of his homeroom.

Elizabeth had mentioned to Conner the other day that he should try to talk to Andy—something about how Andy had news that he'd probably want Conner to hear from him. But Conner wasn't up for lame gossip—and if it was something important, Conner was sure Andy would have talked to him by now.

I just want to sit in a desk and sleep, Conner thought, rounding the corner of the hall. *Yeah. Sleep would be good.* He was nearing his homeroom door when he felt someone tap him. *Not again.* This was more than he could take.

Conner turned, and there was Tia, staring up at him with wide eyes. Was she going to get on his case too? Because it was the last thing he needed. "What?" he snapped.

Tia flinched. She grabbed onto her silver ring and began to twist it around and around her finger. Then she dropped her arms by her sides. "Nothing. I mean, I just wanted to talk."

Hadn't they covered this? They were *not* going to be involved. Period. Did Tia really want to go over it all again? And he'd already apologized for the other night. What more did she want? Conner felt like he was about to snap.

"We already talked," he told Tia stiffly. Conner was starting to turn back around when Tia grabbed his arm. *Hard.*

Conner glanced at her, and she let go.

"I *wanted* to talk about Angel," Tia said, her voice shaky and her big, round eyes narrowing into slitted ovals. "About the fact that he has a new girlfriend and how much that hurts. I thought I could talk to my *best friend* about it. But I guess I was wrong." Tia glared at him for a moment longer, then stormed off, stalking right past Conner and into their homeroom.

Conner scrunched his eyes shut. *Angel? New girlfriend?* He opened his eyes and kicked at the row of lockers, causing a clanging sound to reverberate down the hall.

You are such a jerk, McDermott.

Wonderful. Conner had only been awake for an hour, and already this day sucked.

"Do you think we'll have to live in the dorms?" Melissa Fox asked Will Simmons during lunch that day in the cafeteria. "'Cause some schools make freshmen do that."

Will smiled across the table at his girlfriend. She looked so cute when she scrunched up her nose that way. As if living in the dorms was the equivalent to buying your entire wardrobe at Kmart or something. Okay, so Melissa was picky. And even slightly snobby. But Will loved that about her. He couldn't help it.

"No way. Wherever we go, I'll be on a football scholarship," he reminded Melissa. Will leaned back in his seat, stretching his hands behind his chair. "And athletes are treated like kings. They'll definitely let us live off campus."

Melissa's clear blue eyes lit up. Her *entire face* lit up.

"Together?" Cherie Reese piped in, her pouty little mouth dropping slightly open.

Will and Melissa locked eyes, sharing a smile. Will couldn't wait to live with Melissa. It was the perfect next step for their five-year relationship to take.

"Of course," Melissa told her friend.

Gina Cho, who was sitting on the other side of Melissa, frowned at the roll she was in the process of buttering. "What are you going to tell your parents, Liss?"

"That I want to live with Will," Melissa stated simply, picking the chunks of avocado out of her salad. "They practically love him more than they love me. They won't care. In fact, they'll be psyched."

Will grinned again as he took a huge bite of his

sloppy joe. Melissa was right. *See?* This was all going to work out so perfectly. He knew it.

Cherie leaned her pale elbows on the long, white table, dropping her head in her hands. "You guys are already figuring out where to live, and I don't even know where I'm applying." She moaned.

Will shook his head, putting down the remains of his messy sandwich. "Neither do we." He hated it when Cherie whined. It was so . . . annoying. "I mean, we have an idea, but we're going to see what scouts come around to see me first." A wave of pride rushed through Will as he said the words. Plenty of scouts had already showed interest in him. And he *did* feel sorry for people like Gina and Cherie, who didn't have athletic talent like him or superior grades like Melissa to ensure their acceptance into a top college. But for Will and Melissa, this was going to be cake. No doubt.

Gina pushed her orange plastic tray away from her, pulling her straight, dark hair up into a ponytail. "What happens if you guys don't get into the same school?"

"We will," Melissa responded coolly. She took her blue cardigan—the one that matched her eyes—off the back of her chair and draped it across her narrow shoulders. "The scouts that have been coming by so far are all from good schools," she explained, echoing Will's thoughts. "And our top choice is USC. We both should definitely get in there."

Will raised his eyebrows. "Don't forget about

Michigan, Liss," he reminded her. And how could she? he wondered. They had gone over all of this last night after Will had learned that the scout from the University of Michigan—a school he was definitely psyched about—was going to be at the Sweet Valley practices this week.

There Melissa went with her nose scrunching again. Only this time Will didn't find it so cute. "But Michigan's, like, subzero weather all the time," she complained, listlessly pushing her salad around on her plate. "Besides, USC is close to home."

"And it'll be closer to me," Gina added. "I'm only applying to state schools."

Will rolled his eyes. He liked Gina and all, but being near her was *not* going to be a deciding factor in where he went to college. "But Michigan's *the* school for football," Will argued. "And I thought we decided we were ready for a real change, remember?"

Melissa's light eyes opened wide as she delicately wiped the corners of her mouth with a napkin. "A change, yes. But being in the middle of nowheresville? Don't you think that's a little much?"

Will sighed, exasperated. He ran a hand through his blond hair, leaning forward on the table. "No. Not when you're at an enormous university."

"You guys?" Cherie put in suddenly, sharing a wary look with Gina. "You have plenty of time to argue about this. Why don't you at least wait and see where you get in first?"

41

Will glanced at Cherie, surprised. For once in her life, the girl had said actually something intelligent. Will didn't even know if the Michigan scout was going to like him or not. Cherie was right. He might be arguing for no reason.

Will reached across the table and took Melissa's hand in his. "Yeah," he said, looking into her eyes and squeezing her hand. "Okay."

The corners of Melissa's mouth curved into a smile. Will slumped back into his seat, relaxing.

He'd stop fighting for now; no problem. But if Will was accepted at Michigan, the arguments were *not* going to stop.

Not until Melissa agreed with him.

Thank God we're here, Conner thought as he crunched down on an ice cube.

Okay, so maybe the plastic picnic table on Lucky Burger's concrete patio wasn't exactly paradise. The overwhelming grease from the crispy onion rings *was* currently settling uneasily in Conner's stomach, and the intense midday sun was beating down on his face, causing beads of sweat to form on his forehead. But at least he and Elizabeth were outside the airless, suffocating confines of Sweet Valley High. And *that* was a major relief.

Conner watched Elizabeth as she gingerly scraped the neon orange "special sauce" off her Chicken Deluxe sandwich, grateful that he had been able to convince her to leave the school grounds for lunch.

That was about all Conner felt grateful for today. He knew he'd been a jerk to his friends this morning, but there wasn't much he could do about it, seeing as he still didn't have the patience to talk to any of them. He was too tired. Too moody. And way too anxious.

Conner pushed his half-eaten lunch away from him. Usually he'd finish an entire double cheeseburger in seconds. But the fact that his nerves were engaging in battle in his stomach was making digestion a little difficult.

Conner was still thinking about last night. And about how long it had taken him to sound decent. How much *vodka* it had taken. *What if I completely bomb out on Friday?* he thought, wiping his sweaty palms on his jeans. This was Conner's big chance to play in front of a new crowd in a cool space. What if he blew it?

Elizabeth reached over and placed a hand on Conner's leg, stopping it from bouncing up and down. Conner hadn't even realized that he'd been moving his leg at all.

"Hey." She stared into his eyes. "You nervous about Friday?"

"What?" Conner scratched the back of his head, not sure if he could deal with letting Elizabeth in on what was going through his brain. On its own accord, his leg started to bounce up and down again.

Catching himself, Conner quickly halted it. *Might as well tell her,* he thought. Elizabeth usually seemed to guess what he was thinking anyway. "Yeah. I guess."

Elizabeth pushed aside her chicken sandwich so that she could lean forward on the table, bringing her legs onto the bench and sitting up on her knees. "Conner, I know that you think I only said you were good last night because I'm going out with you."

Conner felt a blush start to creep up his neck. The girl was a freakin' mind reader. Conner moved his focus away from Elizabeth's blue-green eyes to the silver, heart-shaped necklace that hung against her collarbone, unsure of what his own eyes might reveal to her.

Elizabeth bit her lip. "But that's not true," she went on, slapping her hand down on the table to punctuate her point. "You really were amazing. And I'd definitely think so even if you weren't my boyfriend." Conner allowed himself to meet Elizabeth's gaze again. She broke out into a small smile, her eyes twinkling. "But then, of course, I'd want you to be."

Conner stared back at her, feeling a calming rush of relief. Relief that Elizabeth understood without him having to explain. Relief that she really did think he had talent and that he was able to believe her. Sort of. But sort of was better than nothing.

Conner leaned forward over the picnic table. Cradling the back of Elizabeth's head with his hand, he kissed her, running his fingers through her thick blond hair. His skin tingling, he felt like he could just stay here forever. Kiss her forever.

Moving his lips to Elizabeth's soft earlobe, Conner gruffly whispered, "Thanks."

And suddenly Conner felt more grateful than ever. For Elizabeth. If she was all Conner had to be grateful for, then fine.

Elizabeth was enough. She had to be.

Andy Marsden

To: adesmond@stanford.edu
From: marsden1@swiftnet.com
Subject: What's the news?

   Hey. How's it going? How's Stanford? Life in general?

   So, I heard you're seeing someone. What's the story? Who is she? Don't mean to be nosy, but you know me. I just gotta know.

   Oh—and I have news for you too. Whenever you have a moment.

   Peace.

Angel Desmond

To: marsden1@swiftnet.com
From: adesmond@stanford.edu
Subject: The news

Andy:

Good to hear from you. It's been a while. Things are all right here. Finally getting adjusted to dorm life, the workload, etc.

Well . . . her name's Monica. Met her in my comp-sci class. Things are going well so far, but who knows.

I feel horrible about Tia. The last thing I wanted to do was hurt her. But I had to be honest. What do you think I should do?

Hey, what's this big news? I'm all ears.

Take care. And watch after Tee for me, okay?

                                    Angel

Andy Marsden

To: adesmond@stanford.edu
From: marsden1@swiftnet.com
Subject: The news can wait

Don't worry about Tee. She was definitely bummed out, but you did the right thing. It would've been worse if she heard from someone else. She just needs to get over the shock—she'll be okay. And of course I'll look out for her (don't I always?).

Regarding my news—why don't we wait until we see each other to talk about it—or at least talk on the phone. It's not exactly an e-mail kind of conversation.

Later.

CHAPTER 4
Beyond Immature

"God. I wish practice didn't go so late." Tia groaned as she pulled her backpack out of her locker after cheerleading on Tuesday afternoon. "Davidson gave us a ton of reading to do tonight."

Jade pulled her eighties-style red Adidas windbreaker on over her white, V-neck T-shirt, rolling her eyes. "It's not like you actually have to do it, Tee. I mean, Jess and I always fake our way through his class," she said, shooting a look at Jessica, who was in the middle of brushing out her shoulder-length blond hair.

But Jessica didn't even acknowledge the comment. Putting down her minibrush on the locker-room bench, Jessica simply opened her oval compact and checked out her reflection from all angles without saying a word.

Jade raised an eyebrow. Jessica had been acting totally weird lately . . . ever since Jade had started to show interest in Jeremy. In fact, Jessica had barely even spoken to Jade since then. And when she did, her responses were always forced. It was *so* lame. Well, Jade wasn't going to just stand there and take it.

"Right, Jess?" she asked, placing a hand on her hip as she waited for a response.

Jessica glanced at Jade, snapping the compact shut. "Yeah. Right," she said, tossing the brush and mirror in her black leather backpack.

Again Jade rolled her eyes. This was beyond immature. Jessica and Jeremy had been over for weeks. And Jessica had dumped *him*. She had no right to be upset that Jade was seeing Jeremy. But apparently she was.

She's just going to have to get used to it, then, Jade thought, closing her locker door. And there was no time like the present for Jessica to get with the program. Jade picked up her messenger bag, slinging it over her shoulder, and looked back at her friends. "Hey. I haven't had a chance to tell you guys about my night with Jeremy," she began breezily.

Annie Whitman, who was getting dressed next to Jade, raised her eyebrows in obvious surprise. "You went out with him again? Already?"

Jade smiled, gathering half of her straight, dark hair up into a sunflower barrette. "Uh-huh. And this time was better than last."

Jade caught Tia casting a worried glance Jessica's way, but Jessica didn't react. *Good,* Jade thought. *Keep your problems to yourself.*

Jessica cleared her throat as she zipped up her black hooded sweatshirt. "So . . . what did you guys do?" she asked, clearly trying to sound nonchalant.

"Let's see. . . . First he took me to this park in El

Carro that has killer views of the sunset," Jade began, walking toward the locker-room door. Tia, Annie, and Jessica all followed her. "And *then* we went to some little shack off the beach that had these awesome fried-fish sandwiches and potatoes."

"Sounds low cal," Annie remarked sarcastically as Jade pushed open the locker-room doors.

Jade laughed. "It definitely wasn't," she responded, stepping onto the linoleum floor of the near-empty lobby. "But it *was* fun." She stopped walking and let her eyes rest on Jessica for a moment, daring her to say something negative.

And for a brief moment it almost looked like Jessica just might. Her bluish green eyes darkened, and her mouth stiffened into a straight line. But then Jessica quickly glanced away, focusing on nothing in particular and biting her lip.

"*Okay*, let's get going already," Tia broke in suddenly, cutting the thick silence. She hooked her arm through Jessica's, pulling her toward the heavy doors that led outside. "Didn't I just say I have tons of homework?"

Tia and Jessica opened the doors and headed out. Jade followed slowly, satisfied.

Good. Jessica's getting it through her brain that I'm with Jeremy now, she thought, relishing the way the cool evening breeze whipped through her hair. Jade began to jog down the steps, feeling light and free. *The sooner she accepts that, the better.*

* * *

Glad I chose the day that the Michigan scout came to totally choke, Will thought miserably, buttoning up his striped shirt as the usual postpractice locker-room sounds exploded all around him.

All right. Maybe he hadn't *completely* choked. But he'd messed up that one pass pretty badly. Will dropped down on the narrow wooden bench, lacing up his sneakers as his stomach twisted and turned with anxiety. The thing was, he hadn't expected to get that shaken up. That nervous. When he'd played in front of other scouts, he had performed almost without flaws. But of course, when the first school that Will *really* cared about arrived, he freaked out.

Good-bye, Michigan, Will thought, dragging himself up. At least Melissa would be happy.

"Did you catch how short Tanya Bennett's skirt was today?" Jake Collins, Will's teammate, called out to all the guys who were getting dressed in their row of lockers.

"Collins." Todd Wilkins shook his head as he shrugged on his jacket. "The girl is a *freshman*. Are you gonna rob the cradle or something?"

Will quickly grabbed his backpack off the floor and shouldered it, bolting toward the door. He was definitely not in the mood for the typical locker-room banter today.

"Later, Simmons," Todd called after him.

Will waved a hand without bothering to turn around. As he pushed open the metal locker-room door, he tried to figure out how he could let his confidence get so shaken. *You still have a few more days to show the guy,* Will reminded himself, staring down at the not-quite-white, not-quite-a-color lobby floor as he walked. *You just need to stay focused.* Will pushed open the front doors and stepped outside. *Pretend he's not there.*

"Mr. Simmons!"

Will's shoulders jumped, and he turned slightly, startled. His eyes widened when he saw that the person who had called his name was none other than the Michigan scout.

Perfect. He was probably going to tell Will to forget about Michigan altogether.

"I've been looking for you," the guy continued, walking over to Will before he had a chance to respond. "Hank Krubowski. University of Michigan." He held out a hefty hand.

Will's nerves shot into overdrive as he shook the guy's hand. He immediately put on his best smile. "Yeah, yeah. I know."

Hank crossed his arms over his chest and stared down at Will, his blue eyes focused and intense. Hank was a good deal taller and bigger than Will— Will had never felt so small in his life. "That was some good playing out there today."

What? Will tried not to show his surprise. Had the guy blinked or something during Will's terrible pass? Will licked his lips, shifting his weight from one foot to the other. "Thanks."

"No. Thank *you*." Hank swung an arm over Will's shoulders, leading him toward the steps. "Do you have a moment to talk?" he asked, tipping his head toward the parking lot.

Did he? Will would've dyed his hair pink if the guy asked. "Sure. Of course."

"Great. Great." Hank nodded, dropping his arm. He headed down the steps, motioning for Will to follow. "So. I heard your old school got destroyed by an earthquake."

Suddenly Will's hopes soared. Hank had done research on him? Obviously he was at least a little bit interested in Will. Maybe he hadn't played quite as badly as he'd thought. . . .

"Oh, yeah. Last year," he responded, dumbfounded, following Hank into the parking lot.

Hank shook his head, running a hand through his thinning, dark brown hair. "That's gotta be tough. Switching schools your senior year."

Will moved the weight of his backpack from his right shoulder to his left, trying to comprehend that he really was casually conversing about himself with the Michigan scout. "It was."

Hank stopped in front of a mud-splattered, dark blue station wagon. He smiled broadly. "Well, Mr. Simmons, it seems like you've managed all right."

Will glanced down and kicked at the asphalt, basking in the compliment, his heart pounding.

"Anyway. I'll cut to the chase so that you can go

on home and get started on your homework." Hank leaned against the car, crossing one huge leg over the other and sticking his hands in his khakis' front pockets. "I'm sure you've been getting visits from scouts all over the country," he ventured, peering into Will's face with those intense eyes.

Will scratched his forehead. What was the protocol here? Was he supposed to tell the truth or what? "Sort of," he admitted.

"Figured as much. But I want you to know, I think Michigan could be the perfect fit for you."

Will's pulse began to race at Mach speed. This couldn't be happening. Not to him. The guy was trying to sell him on the school! Clearly he wanted to get him in, right?

Hank leaned down and unlocked the driver's-side door. Will tried to hold in his excitement as Hank crawled his bulky frame into the car, reaching for something. When he pulled himself back out, he was holding a shiny, royal-blue-and-yellow folder.

"Now, I'll be here all week, so we'll have plenty of time to talk," Hank explained, pointing at Will with the folder. "But why don't you read this information packet tonight? You can ask me any questions you have tomorrow, all right?"

Will took the folder in his hands, grasping it tightly. "Yeah. Sure. Of course."

"Okay, then. See you tomorrow?"

Will nodded excitedly. He knew he must look like

an idiot, with his head bobbing up and down like a puppet's, but who cared? "Tomorrow," he agreed.

Hank got into his car, and Will waved the folder at him. As Hank slammed the door and started up the car's engine, Will turned, heading for his own car.

It took everything in him not to gallop. But Will did break into a jog, eager to get home as soon as possible. After all, he had some amazing news to spread. Not to mention some serious convincing to do.

Michigan was trying to recruit *him!* It was a dream come true.

Actually, he could try to find Melissa now, Will realized, taking a moment to glance around the lot. The cheerleaders might still be here.

Then Will decided against it. He needed a few minutes to absorb this, to relish the excitement of the moment. Then, after he'd allowed himself to come down to earth, he'd think it through. Figure out how he should present his case.

When Will reached his car, he glanced down at the folder, breaking into a huge smile as he stared at the big yellow *M* in the center of the cover. Now that this was in his hands, nothing was going to stop him.

You're going to love Michigan, Liss, he thought, his eyes lighting up. *I'm sure of it.*

A plan was beginning to take shape in Jade's mind.

She was swinging her keys around as she approached her black Nissan after cheerleading practice, congratulating herself on being so brilliant. Jade had just decided that she would buy Jeremy a little gift. *Or maybe I'll write him a cute note,* she amended. Jeremy was definitely the type to appreciate something like that.

Jade was stepping closer to her car, working out the details in her brain, when she heard Cherie's whiny voice coming from behind her.

"I mean, I *could* get the black dress. But everyone wears black, you know?"

Jade let out a sigh, stopping in front of her driver's-side door as Lila, Cherie, Gina, and Melissa strolled past her.

"Bye, Jade," Melissa said, a saccharine-sweet smile pasted on her face. Melissa and the three other girls were heading toward Lila's car, which was parked right next to Jade's.

Jade forced a tight grin. "Bye." It was bad enough that she had to see these snobs at practice every day. She did *not* enjoy having extra conversation with them on top of it. Annoyed, Jade unlocked her car and opened the door.

"Hey, Wu. Bolting out of here?"

Jade glanced up to see Josh Radinsky heading her way. She stood, leaning her arms on her open car door and slowly smiling. Josh was so good-looking. Brad Pitt good-looking. "Is there any reason I should stay?" she responded lightly, twirling a strand of hair around her finger.

Josh shrugged as he walked closer. "I don't know. Maybe to have the pleasure of talking to me for a couple of minutes?"

Jade laughed, staring up into Josh's hazel eyes. "I'm not sure that's really enough of a reason."

Josh nodded, pretending to think this over. "Okay. How about so I can tell you that you look totally gorgeous today?"

Jade's eyes widened as she beamed back at Josh. She was just about to come out with a perfect flirty response when Lila stiffly called out, "Hi, Josh."

Josh and Jade both turned to look at her. Lila was just standing there in front of her car, *staring* at them. As if they'd committed a crime or something. Lila was also sure to give Jade an extra-special look: the death glare.

Please. What was *with* everybody? Was Jade supposed to care that Lila had gone out with Josh at one point in her life? Didn't anybody move on anymore? Jade never tried to claim ownership of any of *her* exes. Besides, she and Josh were only talking. *Not that it should matter.* Jade wrapped her hand around her car keys, gripping the jagged metal tightly.

"Hey, Lila," Josh said, jutting out his chin. Then he turned right back around to look at Jade.

Ha. So there.

Josh ran a hand through his thick, wavy brown hair. "Anyway. You ready for that Spanish test on Thursday?"

Jade could feel Lila's eyes trained on her. *Could this girl please get a life?* she wondered. "Not really," she said, shrugging.

The corners of Josh's mouth curved into a smile. His eyes ran the length of Jade's body, obviously checking her out. "That makes two of us. Do you want to come over tomorrow night? To study?"

Jade arched an eyebrow. That mention of studying sounded like it was an afterthought, didn't it? Somehow Jade didn't exactly think that if she went over to Josh's, work would be the top thing on his mind. Not considering the way he was looking at her right now.

The question was: Did Jade care? And was she up for it? Jade chewed on the inside of her lip. Of course, there was also Jeremy to consider. But he and Jade were just hanging out. It's not like they were boyfriend-girlfriend. It's not like they were serious.

Jade snuck a quick glance in Lila's direction out of the corner of her eye. Lila was still watching, pouting— why not give her something to really be upset over?

Jade smiled. There. Decision made.

"Sure," Jade told Josh. "Why not?"

Jeremy dragged himself out of his car in House of Java's parking lot at six-thirty that evening, wishing more than anything that he didn't have to work. *But you do, Aames. No getting around it.* Sighing, Jeremy locked the driver's-side door and walked toward HOJ's entrance.

Normally Jeremy wasn't much of a complainer. But today had been an excruciatingly long day. He'd had pop quizzes in *two* of his classes (both of which he'd probably failed), had gotten into an idiotic fight with his friend Stan over a silly homework assignment, and had an extra-long football practice. He'd had just enough time to drop off his backpack at home and wolf down a peanut-butter-and-jelly sandwich before coming here.

Maybe it won't be busy tonight, Jeremy thought hopefully as he neared HOJ's glass doors. *Maybe it'll be an easy shift.*

Maybe not. Jeremy pulled open the door and was met not only with the overwhelming aroma of brewing coffee, but also with the buzzing din of the huge crowd packed inside. Every available chair, overstuffed sofa, and table seemed to be taken. Jeremy glanced around, taking it all in. It was a *Tuesday* night. What were all of these people doing out anyway?

"Aames, I've never been so glad to see you, man," Danny, Jeremy's coworker, called from the espresso machine as Jeremy trudged over to the counter. "Corey left fifteen minutes early, and I am getting *crushed.*" Danny ran a hand over his short, blond crew cut. He turned around to hand a middle-aged woman a short latte.

"Yeah. I can see. Just give me one second," Jeremy responded, heading for the back. But Danny didn't even seem to hear him. He was already taking the next customer's order.

Jeremy sighed again as he opened the flimsy wooden door that led to the stockroom, the manager's office, and the "staff lounge"—a small room with a used maroon sofa stuck in the corner. When Jeremy walked inside, Ally Scott, HOJ's manager and the owner's daughter, was sitting at her usual spot behind the beat-up old desk, doing paperwork.

"Jeremy," she said without glancing up. "Thank God you're here. It's a mess out there, isn't it?"

Jeremy nodded as he opened the door to the staff closet. "Total." He pulled out his green apron, thinking that if Ally weren't sitting there, he would definitely take a couple of minutes to hide out before starting his shift. But that was clearly not an option. "Later," Jeremy said, holding on to the apron and heading back outside.

"Make sure all the milks are full!" Ally yelled as he walked through the door.

Jeremy shook his head. As if he ever *didn't* make sure the milks were full. He was headed for the milk-and-sugar station about to do just that when he noticed that there was a folded-up piece of paper pinned to his apron. For a moment Jeremy was about to turn around to go back to the closet, figuring that he had accidentally taken someone else's uniform. Then he noticed that his name was neatly printed on the piece of paper in small letters.

Curious, Jeremy stopped in place and quickly unpinned the note, unfolding it.

Hi, Jeremy. Just wanted to tell you what an amazing time I had last night. I loved the view . . . and everything else. Call me later.

Jade

Wow. Jeremy's entire body filled with a soothing warmth. He was beyond touched that Jade would go out of her way to do something so sweet. So cool. *She must've dropped this off on her way home from practice,* he realized, rereading the note.

Jeremy's cranky mood dissolved in an instant. How could he be down when he was going out with such a thoughtful, incredible girl? *It's so awesome that she doesn't play games,* he thought, neatly folding the note back up and dropping it into the front pocket of his white button-down shirt. *She just says what's on her mind.* Most girls would be afraid to do something so bold, not wanting to appear overeager. They didn't realize that guys completely appreciated little reaffirmations like this.

But Jade totally gets it. Jeremy smiled to himself, psyched. Right then and there he decided that he was going to do something cool for Jade in return. She deserved it. Jeremy's heart jumped. It was hard to believe, but this thing between them was definitely going somewhere.

"Yo, Aames! Are you going to help me out here or what?"

Jeremy glanced over at Danny, who was dealing

with a line of customers that practically went out the door. Jeremy quickly tied on his apron, rushing over to help. "Sorry, man. What do you need?"

"A tall decaf espresso and two grande skim cappuccinos."

Jeremy nodded, pressing the red button on the espresso machine, suddenly energized. So he had to work. Big deal. Jeremy could handle it.

After getting that note from Jade, Jeremy could handle just about anything.

Jade Wu

<u>How to Get a Guy's Interest . . .
and Keep It</u>

- Be direct—yet mysterious. Make him wonder.
- Appear to be very busy. You have just enough time in your schedule to talk to him for a few minutes.
- Flirt subtly. Don't be overeager—then you just look desperate.
- Make sure he realizes that plenty of guys like you.
- Give him something. That way he's constantly reminded of you.

Josh Radinsky

<u>How to Get a Girl's Interest</u>

-Tease her. Make her laugh.
-Dress well.
-Make sure she knows that plenty of
  girls are into you.
-Take her somewhere cool.
-Flirt, flirt, flirt.
-Did I mention flirt?
-Oh, yeah. And a private basement
  with a thirty-six-inch TV screen
  doesn't hurt.

CHAPTER
5 Some Sort of Sick Joke

"Jade Wu? Is there a Jade Wu here?"

Damn. Jade had just managed to drift off into sleep in the uncomfortable position of her head flat against her wooden desk as she waited for homeroom to start when she was rudely awakened by someone calling her name.

"She's right here," Jade heard Jessica, who was sitting across the room from her, say.

Thanks, Jess, Jade thought, opening her eyes. Of course Jessica would have to give her away. She was acting like such a brat lately. What did they want anyway? *It better not be the principal's office,* Jade thought, slowly lifting her head. *Because I just can't deal if—*

Jade's inner tirade stopped short. Standing before her desk was a tall, skinny delivery guy, carrying a bouquet of *flowers.*

"Ms. Wu?" the guy said. "These are for you."

For me? Jade broke out into a huge smile. *Flowers?* Someone had sent her flowers in *homeroom?* This was too cool. Jade sat on the edge of her chair, speechless, as the guy placed the bouquet, which was arranged in a small glass vase, down on Jade's desk. As Jade leaned over to smell the pink and yellow flowers, she noticed that the entire room had fallen silent. And everyone was staring at her.

Jade was in heaven.

"If you could just sign here . . ." The guy placed a white paper in front of Jade.

"Of course." Jade grabbed her Barbie pen from her bag and happily signed her name on the appropriate line.

"Thanks. Enjoy," the guy said, taking the piece of paper and tipping his purple Lakers baseball cap before walking out.

Oh, I will, Jade thought, leaning over to smell the flowers again, aware that everyone was still watching her. Jade made sure to milk it for all it was worth. After all, things like this didn't exactly happen every day, did they?

"*So?* Who are they from?" asked Kendra Clark, the girl who was sitting in the desk to the left of Jade's.

"Good question." Jade reached for the little white envelope that was stapled to the bouquet's pink-tinted cellophane wrapper. Of course, Jade had a very good idea who these flowers were from. She only hoped she was right.

Jade could feel Jessica's eyes boring into her as Jade took her time opening the envelope. Out of the

67

corner of her eye she also noticed that Josh, who was sitting just a couple of seats away from her, was looking mighty curious as well. *Aha.* That meant this little treat wasn't from him. That narrowed it down quite a bit. Unless Jade had a secret admirer, these flowers had to be from—

Jeremy. Jade leaned back in her chair, twirling a strand of hair around her finger and biting her lip as she read the words he'd written on the little white card.

> Jade: Hope these start your day off right.
> I got your note, and I just wanted you to
> know that I'm thinking of you . . . a lot.
> Jeremy

Jade smiled again, touched. She also congratulated herself on a job well done. Clearly Jade had calculated right about leaving that little note on Jeremy's apron. Still, even she hadn't imagined that *this* would be the result. Jade moved to the edge of her seat again, turning the bouquet around and taking it in from all angles. This was, without a question, the most romantic thing anyone had ever done for her.

"Well?" Kendra was now propped up on her knees and craning her neck, trying to sneak a peek at Jeremy's note. "Who?"

Jade glanced up, letting go of the bouquet. She casually slipped the note back in its envelope, shrugging. "Just a guy I'm seeing." Jade didn't need to turn her head to take in Jessica's expression. She was certain that the girl was bursting with jealousy.

Sam Hernandez, who was sitting on the other side of Jade, shook his head. "Man. *That* is a bold move."

"And an amazing one," Bridget Myers added. She was fully turned around in her seat in front of Jade's, admiring the bouquet. "I'd *kill* to have a guy send me flowers in school."

Jade fell back in her seat, stretching out her legs and basking in all of the envious stares and comments that were coming her way. *Jeremy definitely deserves extra points for* this *move,* she thought, playing with her cranberry-beaded choker.

Mr. Stern, Jade's homeroom teacher, rushed into the classroom just as the bell rang. "Morning, class," he called, taking off his brown corduroy jacket and hanging it on the coatrack by the door.

As a few people muttered unenthusiastic "hellos" in response, Kendra dropped a note on Jade's desk.

Jade frowned. *Kendra better not be pumping me for more information,* she thought, picking up the piece of paper. The girl was way too nosy. It's not like they were *friends* or anything. Jade unfolded the note.

Are you still coming over to study tonight or what?

Jade arched an eyebrow as she read over Josh's note. *When it rains, it pours,* she thought, glancing from the note to the flowers. *Nothing like jealousy to get a guy interested.*

Jade glanced over at Josh, who was already watching her carefully. She locked eyes with him and nodded, mouthing the word "yes." Josh immediately smiled, his hazel eyes brightening.

"Ms. Wu? Flowers in homeroom?" Mr. Stern observed, leaning against his desk at the front of the room. "You're quite lucky, aren't you?"

Jade grinned at her teacher and shrugged. But the truth was, she simply had to agree.

She *was* lucky.

Tia threw invisible daggers at the back of Conner's head as she sat behind him in homeroom.

Good thing I don't have real ones, she thought, squinting and focusing on a particularly unruly tuft of Conner's scruffy brown hair. *Because I couldn't trust myself not to use them.*

"Next Thursday night, admissions officers from UCLA and several other top schools will be answering questions in the auditorium . . . ," Mrs. Lorenzo, Tia's homeroom teacher, was saying as she read from a stapled packet of papers.

But Tia barely heard her. She knew that she should *try* to pay attention to what Mrs. Lorenzo was talking about, seeing as it did actually concern her future and everything, but Tia was too busy being angry at Conner.

Tia watched as Conner lazily stretched his arms above his head and yawned. He was a mess, no question. And earlier, when he'd walked into the classroom, Tia had noticed that he looked like total crap. His hair was dirtier looking than usual, his complexion was a sickly pale color, and his eyes were rimmed with red.

Tia forced herself to look away from Conner, glancing down at her American history textbook instead. Picking up her red ballpoint pen, she began to scribble on the book's front cover.

The really messed up part was that even though Conner had been a total jerk to her, Tia still cared about him. And right now she was worried. *Very* worried. *What if he really has a drinking problem?* she wondered, filling in the top part of the *A* in *American* with red ink. *What if he needs help?*

Then Tia dropped the pen, sighing. *Yeah, right. Like I'm going to confront him just so he can snap at me again.* She crossed her arms over her chest, resuming her look of hatred aimed at the back of Conner's head. Besides, even if he did have a problem, Conner didn't deserve Tia's help. Not by a long shot.

But just as quickly as that thought entered Tia's mind, another one argued against it. This was *Conner.* How could Tia *not* help him? She sighed, pushing her long, wavy hair behind her shoulders.

Basically Tia had two options: (1) She could try to

talk to Conner again, even though he would probably insult her more than he already had—if that was possible. (2) She could go on ignoring Conner and his possible alcohol problem. So that if and when Conner hit rock bottom, it would all be Tia's fault.

"Any questions?" Mrs. Lorenzo called out, scanning the class for raised hands.

Yeah. I have plenty of questions, Tia thought, slumping over her desk and dropping her head into her hands.

What I need are some answers.

I don't care that Jeremy is going out with Jade. I don't care that Jeremy is going out with Jade, Jessica recited silently as she topped off a cappuccino with foamy milk. *And I really don't care that he pushed me away when I tried to kiss him. Which means he chose Jade over me.* However, thinking the statements didn't exactly make them true.

Jessica forced a tight smile as she handed a red-haired woman her coffee. "That'll be three twenty-five."

The customer handed Jessica a twenty, and Jessica opened the cash register. As she counted out the change, Jessica thought about how much she hated that she cared about Jade and Jeremy. She really, really did. But she hated even more that Jeremy had sent Jade flowers. *Flowers. In school!* Jessica had tried very hard all day not to dwell on it—especially when she knew that Jade enjoyed her jealousy. But somehow being here at House of Java brought it all back to her. Thinking about the happy new couple was simply unavoidable. *Jade. Jeremy. Jeremy. Jade. Flowers.*

It was all just a little too much to take.

"Here you go," Jessica said as she gave the customer her change. She was grateful that there were no more customers at the moment. Suzanne was in the back on a break, and Jessica had so much on her mind, she could barely concentrate on making coffee. Letting out a heavy sigh, she leaned against the back counter, running a hand through her hair and trying to get a clear head.

The more Jessica thought about everything, the more muddled her thoughts became. And the more frustrated *she* became. *How can Jeremy like* Jade? Jessica thought, pulling her black mock turtleneck away from her neck as she began to feel hot. *She is so not his type.* I'm *his type.*

Jessica grasped the edges of her green apron as she replayed the flower-delivery moment from this morning. The triumphant look on Jade's face. The nausea Jessica had experienced when she'd imagined Jeremy ordering the bouquet from the florist. The memory of what it had felt like to kiss Jeremy, of the way Jeremy had—

Stop! Stop, a voice inside Jessica screamed out. She stood up straight, stepping away from the counter. Remembering all of this was getting her absolutely nowhere. She was going to lose it if she kept on thinking this way.

Shaking her head, Jessica walked over to the side counter by the window, trying to occupy herself by rearranging the Equal packets. Then she glanced toward HOJ's entrance. All of a sudden she wished that a customer would just walk through those doors. Because keeping busy was good. And being left alone to her thoughts was definitely *not* good.

As if someone high above had heard Jessica's request, one of the glass doors swung open. And in walked Lila, sporting a major scowl.

Was this some kind of sick joke? A back-stabbing ex-best friend was not what Jessica had in mind when she'd asked for a customer. Jessica sighed, making her way back behind the main counter. "What would you like?" she asked flatly, placing one hand on her hip.

Lila flipped her long, dark hair over her shoulder. "I didn't come here for coffee," she said. She glanced around the store, making sure no one important was around, then lowered her voice. "You are never going to believe this."

Jessica scrunched her eyebrows together. She knew Lila's gossip tone when she heard it. "What?"

Lila leaned forward on the counter, an angry glint appearing in her brown eyes. "Do you know that at this very moment Jade Wu is hooking up with Josh Radinsky?"

Jessica blinked. And for a split second her heart felt very heavy. *Jade? With Josh?* Then Jessica shook her head. There was no way Lila knew what she was talking about. She was just spreading stupid gossip. And Jessica had firsthand experience with how dangerous *that* was. "Come on. Jade's going out with Jeremy."

"Oh, really?" Lila stood up straight, crossing her arms over her chest. "That might be true. But right now she's over at Josh's on a study date," she stated, making quotation marks with her fingers to emphasize the words *study* and *date*.

Jessica rolled her eyes, wiping her hands on the front of the apron. That was Lila for you. Always expecting the worst in everybody. "Huh. Then they're probably studying, Lila."

"Sure," Lila retorted, pursing her thin, gloss-covered lips together. "Josh Radinsky alone with a girl in that chick magnet he calls a basement? Right. I'm so sure they're *studying,* Jess." Lila shook her head, her expression softening a bit. "Look. I'm only telling you because I know you care about Jeremy. And I think someone should tell him what's going on."

Jessica stared back at Lila, trying to process this. Until recently Jessica would have been sure that Lila was sharing this with her for some hidden, devious purpose—something that Melissa and Lila had thought up to make a fool out of Jessica. But the last time Jessica had talked to Lila, Lila had actually tried to *help* her by giving her advice on Jeremy. And

HAZEL M. LEWIS LIBRARY
POWERS, OREGON 97466

Jessica knew Lila pretty well, even if they weren't friends anymore. She had a strong feeling that Lila was being honest for once.

Okay, Jessica reasoned, fidgeting with her apron's strings. *So maybe Josh wants to hook up with Jade, but that doesn't mean Jade will.* After all, Jade would never do that to Jeremy.

Then Jessica remembered that she herself had gone out with Will Simmons behind Jeremy's back. And if Jessica was capable of cheating, Jade most definitely was.

Suddenly Jessica was angry. And she couldn't lie to herself any longer. She *did* care that Jeremy was going out with Jade. And she also cared that Jade was possibly hurting him.

A lot.

You are a fool, Tia told herself that evening as she cut across her yard to take the back path to Conner's house. *Conner's going to verbally abuse you once again, and you're going to deserve it for hauling your stupid butt over here in the first place.*

Tia pushed back a heavy branch that blocked her way, swearing under her breath as a sharp thorn pricked her finger. Tia just knew that trying to talk to Conner again was beyond idiotic. She was *asking* to get hurt. But Tia couldn't help it. She cared about the jerk. And she was not going to stand back and watch him destroy himself without a fight.

Tia stopped in place, letting out a deep breath as she neared the back of the Sandborns' house. *Okay. You'll just tell him why you're worried straight-out,* she thought, looking up at the darkening night sky. And if Conner assured Tia that he *didn't* have a drinking problem, Tia would at least tell Conner that his attitude had to change. Because right now, it sucked. Big time.

All right. Tia closed her eyes and inhaled some of the crisp, cool air, then resumed walking, marching right around to the Sandborns' front door. Before she could change her mind, Tia rang the doorbell. *Idiot,* she scolded herself one last time, staring down at the concrete doorstep.

"Hey, Tia." Megan smiled as she opened the door. She pushed a strand of her reddish blond hair behind her ear. "Looking for my brother?"

Yes. Because I'm a fool. Tia tilted her head. "How'd you guess?"

"Well, he's not here," Megan said. "You're welcome to come in and hang out with me, though," she teased.

"Tempting. But I actually really have to talk to him." *Because I'm a stupid, stupid girl.* "Where'd he go?"

Megan glanced inside the house, then took a step out. "Crescent Beach, I think," she whispered. "With friends."

Tia raised an eyebrow. *Wonderful.* Crescent Beach and drinking usually went hand in hand. Something told Tia that Conner hadn't gone there to observe the constellations.

At that moment Mrs. Sandborn walked by the doorway. She stopped when she saw Tia and Megan standing on the front step.

"Hello, Tia." Mrs. Sandborn leaned against the door frame, wrapping her pink cardigan more tightly around her body. "Are you looking for Conner?"

Tia locked eyes with Megan, then glanced over at Megan's mother. "Uh, yeah. I am."

Mrs. Sandborn nodded, her face visibly tensing. "Well, when you find him, you can tell him he's in serious trouble. He can't just run out of here on a school night without telling me first."

Tia bit her lip. *Good job, Conner. Why don't you screw up everything at once?* "Sure, okay, Mrs. Sandborn," Tia responded, stuffing her hands in her jacket's front pockets. "I'll tell him. If I find him." She looked over at Megan, who shot her an apologetic look. "Bye."

"Bye, Tee," Megan called after her as she started to walk away.

Stupid, stupid, stupid, Tia thought as she headed back toward home to ask her dad if she could borrow his car. Only now she wasn't using the adjective to refer to herself.

She was most certainly referring to Conner.

Melissa Fox

In order to best assist you in the college-application process, it will be helpful to know what kind of school you're interested in attending and why. Please use the space below to share your thoughts with us.

—Sandy Travis and Peter Maloney
SVH College Advisers

I'm fairly open-minded when it comes to college. Sure, if you asked me straight-out what my top choice was, I'd tell you USC. But I don't <u>have</u> to go there. If it didn't work out for some reason, well, then I'd happily go somewhere else. Because when I think about my future, I know that I need to consider every part of it—not just where I spend the next four years. If I end up going to a lesser school because that's where my boyfriend is accepted, then I'll simply be at the top of my class. That's nothing to complain about. Besides, most schools have honor programs, don't they?

I'm sure you're going to tell me that you should never follow anyone to college. But I don't see why my future with my boyfriend isn't just as important—if not more—as my academic future. What bigger decision is there than choosing whom you're going to spend the rest of your life with? Everything else is meaningless when you compare it to that.

I always have a plan. But in terms of college, I think I'll just wait and see what happens.

CHAPTER 6

NO MORE MS. NICE GUY

If there was one thing Jade knew for sure, it was that there was definitely not going to be any studying going on *here* tonight.

She slipped off her pale blue suede sneakers and curled up her legs on the Radinskys' cushy brushed-cotton couch, glancing around Josh's basement and taking in the unbelievable setup. An enormous big-screen TV sat before her, there was track lighting overhead (which was currently dimmed, no doubt to create a sexy effect), and over to the left stood an intense multilevel stereo system. Jade's eyes widened as they fell on the brass-rimmed glass coffee table, which was covered with remote controls—one for the TV, one for the DVD player, one for the stereo, and one that looked like it controlled the lighting.

Jade smiled and sat back in the couch, cozying into the soft cushions. Yep. This place was make-out central. Which was just fine with her.

"All right. Got our drinks," Josh announced, coming in from the doorway that led upstairs.

Jade glanced over her shoulder and watched Josh

walk in, her pulse speeding up immediately. "Thanks," she responded appreciatively.

It's not that Jade was particularly *interested* in Josh or anything. She truly did like Jeremy. A lot. But there was no getting around the fact that Josh was incredibly hot. Without a doubt, he was one of the best-looking guys at Sweet Valley High. Tonight he was wearing a slate V-neck sweater over a white T-shirt with a pair of perfectly worn-in jeans, and his thick, brown hair was just scruffy enough to look sexy but not totally messy. Basically Josh looked like he'd walked off the pages of an Abercrombie & Fitch catalog.

Jade pushed up the sleeves of her violet boat-neck shirt, observing the fact that Josh probably had a mighty nice body under that sweater. So, how could she pass him up? And why should she? Jade was young. A free spirit. Just because she was seeing Jeremy didn't mean she couldn't kiss other guys. *God*. Life would be so boring if *that* was the case.

Josh set the two soda-filled glasses down on the coffee table, dropping onto the couch next to Jade. "We didn't have any root beer, so I brought down Dr Pepper instead."

Jade raised an eyebrow. "Perfect. I'm a Dr Pepper freak."

Half of Josh's mouth curved into a smile. "Somehow I knew that about you, Wu."

Jade shrugged. She slipped her scrunchie off her narrow wrist, gathering her hair into a bun on top of her head. "I guess I'm just transparent, huh?"

Josh's grin widened. "Hardly." He reached over and picked up one of the remote controls. He hit a button, and suddenly Fiona Apple's soulful voice filled the room.

Jade smirked to herself. Talk about being *transparent*. As if Josh's music selection wasn't a cue to fool around. Amused, Jade reached for the glass closest to her, taking a sip. "So. Are we going to study or what?"

"Oh, uh, yeah."

Jade got a kick out of watching Josh quickly fumble for his Spanish textbook, which was right on the floor next to him. He placed the book on the coffee table, flipping through the pages as he scratched the back of his head. "So . . . what I totally don't get is the subjunctive. I mean, I don't even know what that is in English, let alone Spanish."

"Mmmm." Jade nodded, leaning forward—and closer to Josh—to take a look at the page he was pointing at. She'd go along with this studying charade for as long as he wanted to. Actually, Jade found · it rather entertaining. Who was he kidding?

"I can probably help you with that," Jade told him, massaging her neck. She could feel Josh's eyes on her, and tingles shot up and down her back from anticipation. Jade scooted closer to the textbook . . . and to Josh. So close that she could smell the light hint of woodsy aftershave he was wearing. "But what *I* need to study is the vocab," Jade went on, turning the pages toward the end of the chapter. She knew that Josh was still staring at her. This was good. Very good. "None of these words sound *anything* like English, you know?"

"Yeah," Josh responded, his voice low and gruff.

Jade tilted her head toward him so that she was staring right into his deep-set hazel eyes. "Radinsky," she teased. "Are you gonna look at me or the book?"

Josh's eyes brightened. "I kinda like looking at you."

And then, before Jade even had a chance to blink, Josh's hands were on either side of her face, and his lips were pressing into hers.

Jade gave in, kissing Josh back as goose bumps began to erupt up and down her arms. Josh's kisses were somehow both hard and gentle at the same time, a combination Jade most definitely enjoyed. She lay back on the couch, and Josh fell on top of her, moving on to kiss her neck . . . and then her earlobe.

Jade closed her eyes, smiling, as her body shivered with delight and all of her senses were awakened. There was no question about it.

This was much better than studying.

Tia spotted the crew of guys immediately.

They were huddled in a broken circle on the beach, a few feet away from the crashing waves, flashlights in most of their hands. Tia leaned forward on the steering wheel and squinted, trying to get a better look. Most of the guys had cans of beer in their hands too.

"Of course," Tia grunted, yanking the keys out of the ignition and stepping out of her father's car. She had really wanted to be wrong about Conner's evening activity. On the drive over here Tia had hoped that she would find Conner and company engaged in some sort of nonalcoholic game, like poker . . . or bingo—as unlikely as that was.

The salty wind whipped through Tia's long hair, and she hugged herself as she stomped toward the group, sand streaming into her sneakers. It was chilly out here—at least ten degrees colder than it had been at her house.

The guys' voices and laughter got louder as Tia neared them, and she was starting to be able to make out some faces. She spotted Evan's profile, his longish hair falling over part of his face, and Reese Taylor, one of Tia and Conner's old friends from El Carro. Reese's tall, lanky body was hard to miss even when he was sitting down.

At that moment Reese glanced up and saw Tia walking toward them. "Tee! Hey!" he called, jutting his chin forward in greeting. He nudged Tommy Puett, another old El Carro classmate. "You didn't tell me Tia was coming, Puett."

Hearing this statement, one of the guys whose back was to Tia turned around. It was Conner. And even in the dark Tia could clearly tell that he was annoyed to see her. *Well, the boy is just going to have to deal,* she thought, approaching the group.

Tommy shrugged. "Didn't know. Hi, Tee."

"Hi, guys," Tia said, forcing a smile as she stopped in place right behind Conner. "Heard you were all here and had to come check it out."

Reese lifted his beer up in toasting position. "The more the merrier."

Scott Turner, who had been Tia's seventh-grade boyfriend, nodded. "Yeah. You know you're always welcome, Tee."

Tia glanced at Conner, noticing that his jaw had tightened, signifying his anger. Ignoring Conner's reaction, she looked at Scott. "Thanks."

Scott shrugged and turned around, proceeding to launch into a story that he had obviously been in the middle of when Tia arrived. Conner turned back around as well. *No "hello." Not even a "hey." What a friend.*

"Anyway, you should've seen the *look* on Brian's face . . . ," Scott was saying.

Tia crouched down and tapped Conner. "Can we talk for a sec?" she whispered.

"About what?" he asked flatly, without bothering to turn around.

Tia sighed. "Stuff," she told the back of his head. "Like why you've been so rude lately . . ." Tia hesitated, then rolled her eyes. There was no point in beating around the bush. "And why you've been drinking so much."

Conner quickly swiveled around to face her. His green eyes were cold and distant. "Why don't we

86

talk about why you won't get out of my face?"

Tia clenched her hands into fists. That was it. No more Ms. Nice Guy. "Conner, your mom is going to kick your butt when you get home."

Conner shook his head, letting out a short, annoyed breath. "Scary," he muttered, starting to turn back toward the group.

Tia blinked. *Scary?* Conner wanted scary? Fine. She'd give it to him then.

"Does *Liz* know where you are?" she asked stiffly.

Conner froze. "What?" he asked after a moment. He glanced at Tia sideways out of the corner of his eye. "Is that a threat, Tee?"

There. She got him. He deserved it. And at least he was listening to her now. Tia shrugged, feigning nonchalance. "Maybe."

Conner stared down at his work boots, but Tia could still see the anger flashing across his face. "Tia . . . you say *anything* to Liz," he warned, lifting a hand to emphasize his point, "and our friendship's over."

Stung, Tia stared back at him, stupidly hoping for him to take back his words. But Conner was silent, his jaw set and his green eyes ice cold. And then he turned back to face the group—who were all listening to Scott's story—signaling that their conversation was over.

Tia slowly stood, feeling strangely numb. She was angry, yes. But she wasn't all that hurt. Or surprised. Tia started to walk toward the parking lot, allowing herself one last glance over her shoulder at Conner's back.

Maybe her lack of emotion was due to the fact that Conner's threat didn't seem to hold all that much weight.

After all, Tia was already starting to think that their friendship was finished as it was.

Conner pulled his Mustang into his driveway and cut the engine, feeling surprisingly good. Somehow, even though Tia had performed that annoying little drama-queen scene at Crescent Beach, Conner had still managed to have a fun night with the guys. Listening to his friends' stupid stories had allowed him to escape, to forget about how tense he was about Friday's gig.

Conner opened the car door and let out a small burp. Oh, yeah. And the beer. The beer had definitely helped.

Conner shook his head as he walked toward his front door, remembering the tale that Tommy had shared with the crew tonight. The guy had told some story about scoring with an almost supermodel. *What a joke.* All the guys knew it had been a load. Conner opened the door, walking inside and smiling to himself at the stupidity of his friend's lie. Tommy was utterly clueless when it came to girls. The odds of him hooking up with a gorgeous model were about the same as the sky turning purple. Actually, on second thought, the odds were probably worse than that.

"Conner. Where have you been?"

Conner stopped in place. He glanced to his right and saw his mom standing in the doorway that opened into their living room. Her arms were crossed over her chest, and the corners of her mouth were curved slightly downward. She did not look happy.

Not my problem. "Out," Conner mumbled.

Conner's mother walked toward him, her white terry-cloth slippers scuffling against the unpolished wooden floor.

"Do you have any idea what time it is?" she asked, her light blue eyes narrowing. "And *you know* you can't run out of here without telling me where you're going first."

Conner shoved his hand in his jeans' front pocket. Was she going to pull this every time he went out? It was starting to get old. "I told Megan where I was going," he responded tightly.

Mrs. Sandborn grabbed at her hair with both of her hands, as if to say this was more than she could bear. "*Conner.* We've been over this. As long as you're living under my roof, you have to ask me for permission before going out. Period."

What was this? Conner tried to have one night with his old friends—to relax and unwind—and everyone got on his case! "Why can't you just back off? Just leave me alone already," he snapped.

Mrs. Sandborn's forehead creased into tiny, intersecting lines. Then she peered into Conner's face, her eyes searching. "Have you been drinking?" she asked, her voice slightly softer.

Conner took a step back, putting some distance between him and his mother. "What if I have?"

Mrs. Sandborn's eyes widened. Her round cheeks flared pink. "Conner! This is completely unacceptable! You cannot come in here drunk and expect me to—"

"*Mom*. Back off," Conner broke in. She was such a total hypocrite. Conner glared at his mother, his eyes flashing. "You of all people have no right to lecture me about drinking. *I* was the one who always picked you up at the club when you were too drunk to stand. Remember?"

His mother's mouth slowly closed shut, and her eyes darted to the floor—but not before he glimpsed the tears that filled them.

So he had hurt her. Big deal. She was being impossible. And all Conner wanted to do was go upstairs and fall asleep. He turned away from his mother and began to barrel up the staircase.

"Conner McDermott!" his mother called after him. "You're grounded!"

Conner rolled his eyes as he stormed into his bedroom, slamming the door behind him.

"Do you hear me?" she continued, her voice getting louder as she came upstairs. "Grounded!"

Conner locked his door and dropped down onto his bed. He had heard her, all right.

The point was, he just didn't care.

As far as Jade was concerned, her study date with Josh Radinsky had been wildly successful.

She smiled to herself as she hopped out of her Nissan, replaying some of the moments from tonight in her brain. Moments such as the way Josh had so perfectly, so tenderly kissed that soft spot behind her ear. How he'd told Jade that she was simply *the* hottest girl in school. How Josh had remarked that Jade's gold-hoop belly ring was a total turn-on . . .

Jade quickly unlocked the metal gate to her apartment complex, letting herself in and shutting the gate behind her. Then she hurried across the concrete courtyard over to the front door of her ground-floor apartment.

She couldn't wait to tell her mother about tonight. Jade didn't always share her guy stories with her mother, but she thought her mom would particularly enjoy this one. After all, Josh was a total stud.

Jade opened her front door and stepped inside. All of the lights in the apartment—except for the bathroom light at the end of the apartment's narrow hallway—were off. She walked down the hall, heading toward her mother's bedroom, figuring that she was asleep. Which was just as well. Jade hadn't seen a strange car in their visitor parking space, which meant that her mother wasn't having a "sleep-over date" tonight. So Jade was free to wake her mother up. She knew she wouldn't mind. In fact, some of Jade's favorite childhood memories were of times when she had wakened her mother in the middle of the night to tell her something and had then crawled into bed beside her, sharing her story as the two of them drifted off to sleep together.

"Mom?" Jade whispered, slowly pushing open her mother's bedroom door. "I'm home." Jade opened the door wider and walked inside, stepping softly so as not to startle her mother.

But Jade was being cautious for no reason. Because when she walked up to her mother's bed, all she found was the light gray comforter and two downy pillows.

Her mother wasn't there. She must be sleeping at one of her boyfriends' houses. Or else she'd stumble home at some time in the early morning hours.

Jade stared at the empty bed, trying to ignore the lump that was starting to form in her throat. She did her best to suppress the unexpected, overwhelming disappointment that was welling up inside her.

Jade turned around and traipsed out, letting out a shaky sigh. *I should've just slept at Josh's,* she thought as she wandered into her own room.

It's not like anyone would've cared.

Jeremy Aames

To: jadew@cal.rr.com
From: jaames@cal.rr.com
Subject: Hi

Jade:

Hi. Don't have much to say, really. Just wanted to say hi.

Anyway, how's your night been? What have you been up to? I've just been sitting here trying to finish a stupid English paper.

So . . . when can we hang out again? I heard Conner McDermott's playing at The Shack on Friday night . . . wanna go?

Sleep well.

Jeremy

Jade Wu

To: jaames@cal.rr.com
From: jadew@cal.rr.com
Subject: Hi to you

Jeremy,

Hi. My night wasn't anything special either. Just did homework. But I was happy to get an e-mail from you. And yes, it would be fun to watch Conner. Let's go.

Hope you finish your paper.

Jade

P.S. Thanks for the flowers. They made my day.

A Whole New Understanding

By the following morning Jessica had undergone a complete one-eighty in attitude regarding the whole Jade situation.

I should never listen to Lila's gossip, she thought as she flipped through radio stations while Elizabeth drove her to school. *How stupid can I be? She probably made the whole Josh thing up.*

But a nagging thought lingered in Jessica's mind. *Why* would Lila create that dumb lie? Jessica let go of the Jeep's stereo controls and sat back in the upholstered seat, staring blankly out the window at the passing palm trees.

"You're quiet this morning," Elizabeth observed, pulling into Sweet Valley High's parking lot.

"Huh?" Jessica turned to look at her twin. "Oh, yeah. Just thinking."

Elizabeth nodded as she scanned the lot for a parking space. She spotted one and drove toward it, glancing at Jessica out of the corner of her eye. "Still jealous of Jade and Jeremy?"

"What?" Jessica's mouth fell open. "No!" Her

cheeks heated up, and she looked away, picking at the door lock while Elizabeth parked the Jeep. "I want Jeremy to be happy, that's all."

"Uh-huh. And you don't think Jade will make him happy." Elizabeth shifted into park and turned off the ignition.

"Yes," Jessica responded, then quickly realized how immature she sounded. "No," she amended, moving on to fidget with her silver-link bracelet. She let out a sigh. "I don't know." She had to stop thinking about this, or she was going to drive herself absolutely nuts. That was, if she wasn't nuts already. "Liz? Can we not talk about it?" she asked, lifting up her leather backpack and opening the car door.

Elizabeth shrugged. She pushed a strand of hair behind her ear. "Sure. Whatever you want."

"Thanks." Jessica hopped out of the car, shouldering her bag. *That's it,* she decided, slamming the door. *No more thoughts about Jade and Jeremy. Period.*

Feeling resolved, Jessica walked around the Jeep toward her sister, then the two of them headed for the school entrance. They had taken about two steps when they heard: "Jade Wu was so hot last night. You wouldn't believe it!"

Jessica froze in place as her stomach plunged down to the asphalt. Elizabeth glanced at Jessica, her eyes widening with surprise. Then both sisters swiveled their heads to the left to look at the source of the comment.

Josh Radinsky was standing by his Mazda, bragging to Jake Collins and Ted Masters, another football player. Apparently Josh was oblivious to how loud his voice was. *He probably* wants *everyone to hear,* Jessica thought, disgusted. Suddenly she had a whole new understanding of what the saying "sick to your stomach" meant.

"So did you sleep with her?" Jake asked, rolling forward on the heels of his feet.

Josh clasped his hands, stretching his arms out in front of him. "Well . . . *practically,* if you catch my drift," he boasted, breaking into a huge smile.

"All right!" Ted responded, slapping him five.

"Way to go, Radinsky," Jake congratulated his friend, slapping his hand as well. Ted gave Josh a hearty pat on the back, then all three guys headed off for school.

For a moment Jessica and Elizabeth stood there in silence, absorbing the scene that they had just witnessed. *How could Jade do that?* Jessica thought, her entire body tensing up. *How could she almost sleep with* anybody *when she's going out with Jeremy?*

"God. Guys are so horrible," Elizabeth whispered. "How can they talk about girls like that?"

Jessica turned to look at her sister, her brain still reeling. "*Guys* are horrible?" she repeated, dumbfounded. "What about Jade? Why doesn't she just hook up with Sweet Valley's entire male population while she's at it?"

Elizabeth blinked. "Jessica! You don't even know if what Josh was saying is true." She pulled a tortoiseshell barrette out of her khaki pants' pocket and gathered her hair into a ponytail. "You're the last person who should take some guy's word about something like that."

Jessica felt a blush rise to her cheeks as she flashed back to the beginning of the school year, the rumors about her. . . .

"Besides," Elizabeth added, pulling her ponytail tight, "what Jade chooses to do is her own business."

Jessica couldn't believe it. Her own sister was actually siding with Jade! Over an issue that was more than clear-cut.

"Not if she's hurting Jeremy, it's not," Jessica argued, getting madder and madder by the second. "Think about it. How can she just—" She snapped her mouth shut, breaking off as she spotted Jade in the flesh, locking her car a few feet up ahead.

Elizabeth followed her twin's angry gaze and paled. "Oh, Jess, don't," Elizabeth said, grabbing hold of Jessica's arm. "Don't get involved. This has nothing to do with you."

But Jessica wasn't convinced. "Jeremy is my friend, Liz." She turned to her sister, her aqua eyes narrowing. "It has *everything* to do with me." And with that, she broke free of Elizabeth's grasp and stalked right toward Jade.

Jade's back was to Jessica. She was swinging her

keys around and humming some song as she strolled toward the school steps. Jessica scowled. If what Josh said was true, then the girl didn't deserve to be so happy. And she definitely didn't deserve Jeremy. Then Jessica remembered the flowers, and her anger level reached an all-new high.

"Hey, Jade!" she called tightly.

Jade glanced over her shoulder. "Oh, hi, Jess." She stopped in place, flipping her dark hair from one side to the other. "What's up?"

"Not much." Jessica stomped closer to her. "Except that I just overheard Josh Radinsky saying something interesting."

Jade glanced down, suddenly appearing to be very intrigued by her nails. She picked at her thumb, where the light purple polish was chipped. "Yeah?"

"Yes," Jessica hissed. She paused, crossing her arms over her chest. "He was telling—no, bragging to his friends that you hooked up with him last night."

Jade glanced up from her hands, her black eyes barely registering interest. "And your point is . . . ?"

Jessica's jaw dropped. "*My point is* you're going out with Jeremy!"

Jade nodded, tapping her chin with her finger as she considered this. "Right. Okay. But I still don't see what this has to do with you," she stated. Then she dropped her hand and let out a short laugh. "What? Are you going to tell on me, Jess?"

"What?" Jessica's hands balled into fists. Her neck

felt so tight, she thought it might snap. "Maybe! . . . I mean, you . . . I . . ." Jessica shook her head, as if she was trying to will a coherent sentence to slip out of her brain. Taking a deep breath, she put her hands on her hips and glared at Jade. "Don't you even care that Josh is telling everyone what you did with him?"

Jade shrugged. "I did what I did. And I had fun. So, no, I don't care," she said simply. Jade pulled some lip balm out of her jacket pocket and coated her lips, smacking them together. "And you know what? Neither should you." She put the lid back on the balm and turned around, strolling away as if she didn't have a worry in the world.

Stunned, Jessica watched Jade go.

Was Jessica crazy? Or was she the only person who thought cheating was *not* acceptable?

Nice talking to you too, Tia thought, watching Conner slump out of their homeroom in front of her later that morning.

Tia sighed, pulling her wavy hair out of its ponytail as she stepped out of the classroom and trudged down the hall toward her locker. Apparently Tia and Conner's mutual ignoring sessions were going to continue indefinitely. Conner hadn't even *looked* Tia's way once today.

Tia reached her locker. She threw her nylon backpack down on the floor and reached out to dial her lock's combination. Well, she still wasn't going to give up. Tia might feel like killing the guy right now, but deep down, she cared about Conner way too much to let him simply self-destruct. Besides, Tia was, self-admittedly, a meddler. And this was a situation that called for some serious meddling.

Tia pulled down on her lock, opening it, and then swung open the locker door.

"Hey, Tee. How's it going?"

Liz.

Tia swallowed, staring into her open locker. Last night Tia had decided that part of her meddling strategy would call for her to discuss the Conner problem with Elizabeth. But now, with Elizabeth right behind her, it was the last thing that Tia felt like doing.

Her stomach twisting with dread, Tia turned around and found herself face-to-face with Elizabeth. She sighed. The sooner she got this over with, the better.

"Hi, there," Tia greeted. "Not bad." She glanced both ways down the crowded hall to make sure Conner wasn't anywhere in sight, then looked back at Elizabeth. "Listen. I have to talk to you for a sec."

Elizabeth slipped her backpack off her shoulder and placed it by her feet. "Sounds serious," she said, her eyes narrowing.

"It is. Sort of." Tia bit her lip. She played with her ring, pulling it off and on her finger. *Maybe I shouldn't say anything,* Tia thought, chickening out as Elizabeth waited for her to speak. But at this point that wasn't really an option. Tia had to just come out with it already.

"Have you noticed anything weird about Conner lately?" she blurted out.

Elizabeth paled slightly, her eyebrows furrowing together. "Weird? What do you mean?" she asked, a strange edge to her voice.

Oh, boy. How could Tia explain this one without completely freaking Elizabeth out? And without incriminating herself?

"Uh, hold on a sec," Tia said, crouching down and quickly pulling the books she needed out of her locker. She stuffed the books into her bag, stood up, and slammed the locker shut. "Let's go over here." She walked over to a relatively quiet corner by the stairwell, motioning for Elizabeth to follow.

"Okay, now *you're* acting weird," Elizabeth said, giving her friend a tight, nervous frown. "What's going on?" Elizabeth reached up to fidget with her silver, heart-shaped necklace, and Tia noticed her fingers were shaking slightly.

Tia held back a groan. Obviously Elizabeth wasn't exactly comfortable having a conversation about her boyfriend with Tia yet. So what was Tia supposed to say?

Let's see. I hooked up with Conner behind your back again, even though I said it only happened that one time. And ever since then he's been a jerk. And a drunk. Tia glanced up at the fluorescent lights.

"All right. Here's the thing." Tia cleared her throat,

looking everywhere but at Elizabeth. "Conner's been acting pretty strange to *me* lately."

Elizabeth sighed, a flash of annoyance hardening her features. "Well, there has been *a lot* going on," she said, letting go of the necklace to cross her arms over her chest.

Tia glanced down at the carpeting, feeling the heat rise up to her cheeks. No doubt about what Elizabeth was implying with that little statement. "Right. Okay." Tia looked back up at Elizabeth, hugging her arms to her own chest. "But the main problem is . . . I think Conner's been drinking kind of a lot these past couple of weeks."

"What?" Elizabeth's face went blank, and her eyes widened. "What are you talking about?"

"I know he was drinking one night last week." Tia's eyes darted off to her left, uncomfortable, as she reminded herself of why she knew this: because she had gone over to Conner's house to discuss their kiss. "And, um, he was out drinking beers with a bunch of friends last night."

Elizabeth let out a short, frustrated laugh. "That doesn't sound like so much to me, Tia." Her frown deepened, and Tia could swear she saw a strange hint of accusation in Elizabeth's eyes. "Sure, I wish that Conner didn't drink, but . . . what are you saying? There's something I'm *missing* about *my boyfriend?*"

Tia blinked at the emphasis Elizabeth put on the last two words, then stared at her friend, wondering if she was the only observant person left in southern California. "Haven't you noticed that Conner's eyes are always bloodshot lately? And he always seems tired? I mean, I wouldn't be so worried if his mother wasn't an alcoholic, but—"

Elizabeth's light eyebrows shot up. "Wait a minute," she interrupted. "Are you saying that Conner has a *drinking problem?*"

Bingo. Tia took a breath. "Yes."

Elizabeth's lips parted slightly. Then she let out another tight laugh. "*Tia!* Come on. That's ridiculous!" Tia was about to respond when Elizabeth shook her head and added, "I thought *I* was the paranoid one here."

Paranoid? Now Tia was being called paranoid for the simple act of stating the obvious? She glanced at the floor, her spirits feeling heavy. She wanted to give Elizabeth a major reality check. She really, really did.

But it seemed so pointless. Because apparently Elizabeth was living on the same planet as her boyfriend.

The one called Denial.

The girl must have a serious death wish.

Conner had just walked out of the bathroom and was now channeling an enormous wave of adrenaline that was threatening to overcome him. Because he could see that standing in a corner at the end of the hall were Tia and Elizabeth. And Conner could just *tell* by Tia's intense expression and hand gestures that she was talking about him. That she was telling Elizabeth about last night.

And who knows what else? he thought, his neck muscles tightening. *Man, if she says* anything *to turn Liz against me . . .* Conner grimaced. Tia was doing this just to tick him off. Conner was sure of it.

He began to stalk toward Tia, ready to lay into her. But as Conner nearly bumped into two sophomore girls who were giggling in the hallway, he changed his mind. *No,* he thought, maneuvering his way around the crowds, *I won't give her the satisfaction. That's just what she wants anyway.*

Instead Conner slowed his pace and walked up to Elizabeth and Tia as calmly as possible. He circled his arm around Elizabeth's slender waist and leaned down, giving her a kiss on her soft, lightly tanned cheek. "Hey. Been looking for you," he said.

Elizabeth grinned uncomfortably as he pulled away. "Well, here I am."

Conner didn't even look at Tia, but out of the corner of his eye he could see that she was shifting her weight from one foot to the other.

"Come on," Conner said, moving his arm up to Elizabeth's shoulders and leading her toward the stairwell. "I'll walk you to class."

Elizabeth seemed to relax. Her light eyes softened. "Okay. Good. Bye, Tee," she said to Tia. She paused. "We'll talk later, okay?" she added.

"Later," Tia responded stiffly.

As Conner and Elizabeth started to step away, Conner glanced over his shoulder and saw Tia still standing there, watching them, chewing on the inside of her lip. Which was just fine with Conner. As far as he was concerned, Tia deserved a lot worse. He narrowed his eyes at her, conveying his anger with a death glare, and then turned his head back around, pushing open the door that led to the stairwell.

"Hey, Conner?" Elizabeth began as they made their way down the first flight of stairs. "I, um, have to ask you about something."

Conner's shoulders stiffened. *Here goes,* he thought. "Yeah?"

Elizabeth tugged on his arm, bringing him over to the large window by the stairwell's landing. She stared up into his eyes, smiling slightly. "Tia just told me something, and I know it's completely insane—" She broke off for a moment, glancing down. Then she shook her head and looked back at Conner. "Anyway. *Tia said* you've been drinking a lot lately, which I know is ridiculous, but I was just wondering if you knew why she thought that."

Because she's a crappy friend, Conner thought. He rolled his eyes, running a hand through his hair and letting out a short breath. "Last night a bunch of the guys from El Carro and I got together and had some beers to celebrate Reese Taylor's birthday."

"Oh. Like a party?" Elizabeth asked, her voice sounding somewhat hopeful.

"Yeah." Conner nodded. "Tia tracked us down. She was annoyed that no one had invited her, so she totally lost it. She blew everything out of proportion."

Elizabeth raised her eyebrows. "And that's all?"

Conner shrugged. "That's all. Tee went psycho on us." He sighed, grasping at the ends of Elizabeth's silky hair, stroking it. "I can't believe she bothered *you* about it." Technically that was the truth. Conner couldn't believe anything Tia had done lately.

Elizabeth's eyes brightened. "She probably just needed to vent." Elizabeth stood on her tiptoes, reaching up to give Conner a quick kiss. "I'm sorry I even brought it up," she told him, pulling away.

"Don't be," Conner responded. He placed his hands on Elizabeth's shoulders, massaging them as she turned around and headed for the next flight of stairs.

In Conner's mind there was only one person who should be sorry.

Without a question, that person was Tia.

Will Simmons

To: foxy@swiftnet.com
From: simmons9@cal.rr.com
Subject: Michigan fun facts

Liss:

How's the homework going? I'm procrastinating. Big time.

I was thumbing through Michigan's brochure, and I came across a few tidbits you might find interesting:

It has top-rated English and history departments.

Their cafeteria food is among the best in the country.

The campus is sprawling and beautiful.

Graduates of Michigan consistently get high-paying, satisfying jobs.

Michigan has more school spirit than any other university.

And there's much more. But that's a good start. Right?

Talk to you later.

Love,

me

Melissa Fox

To: simmons9@cal.rr.com
From: foxy@swiftnet.com
Subject: re: Michigan fun facts

Interesting. Let's see now. . . . I don't plan to major in either English or history. I hope to never eat food in the caf, thanks. Does Ann Arbor have good restaurants?

Um, it's so cold in Michigan most of the year that you probably can't enjoy the "sprawling" campus, graduates of USC also get "high-paying, satisfying" jobs, and, well, how exactly do they measure school spirit?

Just wondering.

Love you,
me

CHAPTER 8
Crashing Down to Earth

Jeremy had never had so much fun refilling napkin dispensers in his life.

He smiled to himself as he snapped the metal container shut, then strolled back behind HOJ's front counter, humming the entire time. Jessica cast an uneasy glance his way as she handed a twenty-something customer a double espresso.

Jeremy shrugged. He was happy, all right? He couldn't help it. Jade had said that she'd go to Conner's concert with Jeremy tomorrow night, and he was in a good—no, a great mood. It was that simple.

"That'll be two seventy-five," Jeremy told Mr. Double Espresso, who dug into his baggy jeans' pockets and came up with the exact change. "Perfect!" Jeremy punched open the cash register and stashed away the money. "Have a great evening." The guy nodded and walked away.

Another confused look from Jessica. Actually, now Jeremy noticed that she was staring at him, her forehead wrinkled and her bluish green eyes clouded over. Caught, Jessica quickly glanced away and went

110

back to pouring some of the decaf hazelnut into one of HOJ's purple-and-green checkerboard mugs.

Poor Jess. Jeremy took the next customer's five and made change for him. Jessica didn't look happy at all tonight. *Maybe she needs to meet someone too,* he thought, handing the customer his money and closing the register.

Jeremy dropped his hands into his apron's front pocket, chuckling to himself. *Unbelievable.* He was actually hoping that Jessica—the girl he'd thought he'd never get over—would meet a guy. Life *was* good. Jeremy leaned against the back counter, crossing one ankle over the other. *Thank you, Jade.*

Since there were no more customers at the moment, Jeremy folded his arms over his chest and looked up at the terra-cotta-painted ceiling, allowing himself to drift into thoughts of Jade. Thoughts of her thick, shiny dark hair . . . her flirtatious, teasing laugh . . . her heart-stopping, out-of-this-world kisses . . .

"Jeremy. I have to talk to you."

Jeremy crashed back down to earth to find Jessica standing next to him, her shoulder slumping and her gaze serious and intense. Something was definitely up with her. Jeremy glanced past her at the front door. Still no customers. He stood up straight. "Of course. Shoot."

Jessica let out a sigh. She looked down, seeming to be intently concentrating on her hands. Then she shook her head, dropping her arms by her sides and glancing back up at Jeremy. "Look. I don't know how to say this, so I'm just going to come out and tell you, all right?"

Jeremy ran a hand through his black hair, beyond confused. "Sure. Go ahead."

"Okay." Jessica took a deep breath, momentarily closing her eyes. When she opened them again, her gaze was soft. Apologetic. "Jade is cheating on you."

What? There was no way he had heard her right. It sounded like she had said—Jeremy squinted at Jessica, letting out a tight laugh. "Excuse me?"

She lightly touched his chest. "I'm really, really sorry, Jeremy. But I know for a fact that it's true. She hooked up with someone else."

Jeremy stared back at Jessica, feeling like all of the blood in his body had just frozen over. Feeling his heart drop into his stomach. *Jade? Cheating on me?*

Jeremy took a step away from Jessica, watching as her hand fell back to her side, then turned his back on her. How could it possibly be true? Jeremy reminded himself of Jade's sweet note, of the way she had gazed at him so adoringly at Hyde Park, at how *real* her kisses had felt.

No. There was no possible way. Jade was a no-games kind of girl. Unlike other girls, like—Jeremy turned back around, his shoulders stiffening. Unlike girls like *Jessica,* who lied at the first opportunity they got. *Who'd probably lie to sabotage a relationship that they were jealous of.* Jeremy felt the anger start to rise up in him as he recalled how irritated Jessica had seemed when he and Jade had started to go out.

And how Jessica had even tried to kiss him to get him back, probably just to prove to herself that she could still "win" if she tried.

Jeremy narrowed his deep brown eyes at Jessica. This was an all-new low. Jessica didn't want him—but she didn't want him to be happy with someone else?

"I'm so sorry that I was the one who had to tell you," Jessica babbled, obviously misinterpreting his silence. "It's just . . . I care about you so much, and I don't want to see you get hurt." She stared into his eyes pleadingly, her voice somewhat shaky.

"Jessica, don't even try this," Jeremy snapped, his stomach twisting and turning with anger. "I *know* Jade is not cheating on me."

Jessica paled, and Jeremy let out a short, frustrated breath.

"Man. I can't believe you." He turned his back on her, stalking over to sponge off the main counter.

"You can't believe *me?*" Jessica repeated, following right behind him. "Jeremy, I am not making this up. Ask anyone. It's all over school. She fooled around with—"

"You know what, Jess?" Jeremy turned around, tightening his grip on the bright pink sponge. "Just stop right there. I don't want to hear any more."

Jessica flinched, clearly stung. Her cheeks flamed up. "But Jeremy—"

"Enough!" Jeremy cut her off. Out of the corner of his eye he noticed a few customers turn their way in surprise. Jeremy took a deep breath, then brought his voice down a couple of notches. "I can't believe you'd sink this low."

Jessica closed her mouth, silent. Her eyes began to get watery.

Well, she wasn't going to get any sympathy from Jeremy, that was for sure. Man, he couldn't even *look* at her now. "Just stick to the other side of the coffee-house tonight, okay?" he muttered. "I can't talk to you anymore."

For once in her life, Jessica appeared to be speechless. She stared at Jeremy for a moment longer, then slowly turned, exhaled, and walked away.

Jeremy looked down at the counter, his brain reeling. His stomach felt like he'd just swallowed something that was past its prime.

Sighing, he glanced up and noticed a few customers walk through the glass doors. Suddenly Jeremy felt like he couldn't deal with work tonight.

Of course. Leave it to Jessica Wakefield to destroy my good mood.

I am the man. I am the man! Will was actually *singing* those words to himself as he drove home from football practice on Friday afternoon. He pulled his car to a stop in front of a red light, practically bouncing up and down in his leather seat and feeling like he might jump out of his skin altogether.

Hank Krubowski, the Michigan scout, had taken

Will aside after practice again today. And as unbelievable as it seemed, not only had Hank offered Will a spot in next year's freshman class, but he'd also assured Will that he'd get a *full scholarship* to the university!

Will grasped the steering wheel more tightly, pressing on the accelerator as the traffic light turned green. As he drove, he replayed the conversation he'd had with Hank just minutes before, trying to wrap his brain around the idea that this was all really happening.

"All I can say," Hank had told Will as he'd placed a firm grip on both of Will's shoulders, "is that if you want to attend the University of Michigan, *nothing* will stop you. You're in. Tuition taken care of." When Will had simply blinked back at Hank, stunned speechless, Hank had laughed heartily, slapped Will on the back, and added, "Looking forward to seeing you play in Saturday's game, son."

Now Will smiled to himself, feeling pumped. *Yep.* This was happening, all right. Will was going to Michigan next year, no matter what.

Will reached Melissa's street and swallowed. Well . . . there was *one* matter to be taken care of before Will's attendance at Michigan was guaranteed. *Melissa.* As Will turned down her street, he started to go over all the pro-Michigan arguments in his head. The sports. The spirit. The parties. Oh, yeah. And the academics.

Melissa had to want to go to U of M with Will. He knew she could get in there easily, with her grades. She simply had to. Because college without Melissa didn't make much sense.

Will pulled into the Foxes' circular driveway and cut the engine, psyching himself up. *Just show her how much this means to you,* he told himself, stepping out of his car and jogging up to the front door. *Show her how much this means, and she'll be totally with you.* Letting out a deep breath, Will rang the doorbell.

Mrs. Fox's normally dour-looking face lit up as it always did whenever she saw him. "Good to see you," she said, stepping aside so he could walk in. She motioned to the stairs with a tilt of her head. "She's upstairs. Go on up."

"Thanks, Mrs. Fox." Without hesitating for a moment, Will headed up the immaculately polished, carved-wood staircase.

Melissa's door was already partly open, so Will just opened it wider, stepping inside her bedroom. Melissa was lying stomach down on her bed, chewing on the end of a pencil and reading her American-history textbook, her long brown hair falling over both sides of her face. As always, she looked beautiful. Will only hoped that she was in a good mood.

"Hey, Liss."

Melissa glanced over her shoulder, a full smile on her lips. "Hey. You didn't tell me you were coming."

Will walked over and dropped down on the bed next to his girlfriend, giving her a quick kiss on the cheek as she sat up. "I know. Surprise." Suddenly feeling warm—maybe from all of the excitement—he pulled off his dark blue, V-neck sweater, revealing a gray T-shirt underneath. Then he quickly focused his attention back on Melissa. "I've got another surprise too."

"Really?" Melissa reached up and fixed the part of Will's blond hair that had been messed up when he'd taken off his sweater. Her smooth, wide forehead crinkled as she scrunched her eyebrows together. "What?"

Will stood back up, his nerves feeling newly charged and energized. He beamed at Melissa, crossing his arms over his chest. "You are never going to believe this," he told her, rocking forward on the balls of his feet. "*I* don't even believe it." Will hesitated, allowing a moment for a dramatic pause.

Melissa opened her clear blue eyes wider. "*Well? What is it already?*"

Just be as psyched as I am, Liss. Please be psyched. "Today the Michigan scout told me I was in. *In!* With a full scholarship!"

For a brief moment Melissa was silent, with no visible emotion crossing her fragile features. Will cringed inwardly, praying for a happy response. Then Melissa blinked, sat up on her knees, and said, "Really?"

"Really!" Again Will sat down next to Melissa, grabbing hold of her pale, slender hands and hoping to pass his excitement into her through his fingertips.

"Wow. That's great," she told him, reaching up and giving him a kiss. "Really. Congratulations."

Melissa's arms rested on Will's broad shoulders, her eyes searching his face. "And that's—that's where you want to go?"

Here we go, Will thought. But he wasn't worried. He had prepared for this. *Just be positive,* he told himself. *She'll be with you.*

"Yes! No question," Will responded, squeezing Melissa's hands. He had drawn in a quick breath, about to launch into his sell speech, when Melissa broke free of his grasp and stood, marching straight for her desk by the window.

Uh-oh. What was she doing? Will stood as well, his stomach sinking, as he watched Melissa sort through her pile of papers, obviously looking for something. Will licked his lips, his mouth feeling dry. He knew that Melissa would never break up with him or anything, but what if she was digging up some article about how long-distance relationships really could work? Or some essay proving that Michigan's frigid weather could cause depression? Will cracked his knuckles, suddenly very anxious. What if Melissa refused to apply to Michigan?

"You know that Michigan isn't exactly on my list," she began tauntingly, her back still to Will.

His knees felt like they might give in. *Wait a second.* She wasn't even going to give him a chance to convince her? "Liss, I—"

Melissa turned around, a packet of papers in her hand. She fanned herself with the papers, smiling coyly.

"But lucky for you, I happen to have an application."

Will's gaze fell to the packet. Sure enough, it was stamped with the University of Michigan's official blue-and-gold crest. He smiled as his eyes traveled back up to Melissa's face and caught the obvious amusement in her expression. She was only teasing.

An enormous wave of relief washed over Will. Until this moment Will hadn't realized just how crucial it was to him that he and Melissa be in the same place next year.

"So you'll go?" he asked Melissa, stepping closer to her.

Melissa softly traced the outline of Will's clean-shaven cheek with her finger. "Of course. If that's where you're going to be."

Will closed his eyes. *Thank God.* He leaned down, pulling Melissa into a kiss. A gentle, tender kiss. A kiss that hopefully showed her how important she was to him. As they broke off their kiss, their arms lingered around each other. Will squeezed Melissa tight, hugging her and taking in the light scent of her crisp, sophisticated perfume.

At that second Will realized that for the first time in a while, he knew exactly what he wanted in life. The bonus was, he already had it.

This was the most anxiety-producing night of Conner's life.

And no, that wasn't because he was grounded

and he'd had to sneak past his mom to get out of the house. *What a joke.* Conner rolled down his car window, needing some fresh air. Escaping his mother had been too easy. Cake.

Conner was tense because at the moment, he was driving up the winding mountain road that led to The Shack. In a couple of minutes—before the sun fully set—he'd be at the club. And in less than a couple of hours Conner would be up there on the stage, performing for a larger-than-he-was-used-to crowd.

Conner lifted his foot off the gas, slowing down as he reached the turnoff for The Shack, doubts suddenly overwhelming his brain. He tried to ignore them, but it was useless. A new worry was popping up every second.

What if he choked? What if he froze up onstage? What if he *sucked*?

In a sudden movement Conner cut the wheel, turning in the opposite direction from The Shack and driving up into the near-empty sloping parking lot attached to a run-down-looking building with a sign saying Dale's General Store. Conner had no idea what they sold at Dale's; he just knew that he needed a couple of moments before he'd be ready to walk into The Shack. Some time to unwind. Relax. Chill out.

Conner drove his Mustang behind a Dumpster so that he was out of view from the store, then parked. Without thinking twice he shut off the ignition and reached right for his bottle of vodka, which was tucked under the passenger seat. Conner unscrewed the cap, grateful that he'd planned ahead and thought to bring the bottle with him. Just in case.

Sometimes vodka felt like medicine to Conner. He only hoped that tonight would be one of those times. Conner closed his eyes as he took a big swig, his limbs loosening up almost immediately. Then he dropped his head back against his seat, waiting for the vodka-induced calmness to overtake him.

A moment later Conner popped open his eyes. He sat up. He was still feeling anxious. *Too* anxious. Conner held up the bottle, examining it from all angles, confused. For some reason, the alcohol wasn't working as well as it usually did. *Of course. Just when I need it the most.* Conner quickly downed a few more quick gulps. Thankfully, by the third one, he was feeling all right. Like he could conquer tonight. *Maybe.*

Conner glanced out his window—the one that wasn't obstructed by the Dumpster—and noticed that the sky was starting to turn dark. The sun had set. *Show time.*

Now feeling energized, Conner screwed the cap back on the bottle and stashed it under the seat. He turned the radio all the way up, blasting it, and started up his Mustang, pulling out of Dale's lot.

Conner sped back over to the road he'd been on before, then turned off to the left. The Shack, a single-story, weather-beaten wooden building, was the second building on the street. *You're going to do it; you're*

HAZEL M. LEWIS LIBRARY
POWERS, OREGON 97466

going to kill tonight, Conner silently chanted to himself as he glimpsed the building. *Man.* What had he been so worried about? The audience was going to love him. He was going to put on an awesome show.

Pumped, Conner quickly drove into the lot behind The Shack. A parked station wagon seemed to appear in front of him out of nowhere, and Conner slammed on the brakes, his tires screeching as he came to a sudden stop.

Conner held on to the steering wheel with both hands and dropped his head, his heart racing from the near collision. *Forget about it,* he told himself, trying to shake it off. *Just go in there and save all your energy for the show.*

Letting out a deep breath, Conner shifted the Mustang into park and cut the engine. He stepped out and lifted his guitar out of the car. And as he strolled toward The Shack with his instrument in hand, Conner suddenly felt like a real musician. Like someone who deserved this gig. Basically he was psyched.

Conner entered the club through the back entrance, pushing open the swinging screen door that was right off the manager's office. Once inside, Conner could hear the muted chattering, yelling, and laughing coming from the main hall. Conner glanced at the black-rimmed clock on the wall above the manager's overflowing desk. It was still early. The place was probably half empty. Conner still had plenty of time.

Conner turned and headed for the corner room

across from the bathroom—Chuck, the manager, had referred to it as "the artists' room" the other day. Conner grinned to himself, running a hand through his hair. That's what he was now, he guessed. An artist. Conner's pulse started to race at the thought. His adrenaline was really starting to kick in.

There wasn't much in the room, just a minifridge, a full-length mirror, and a thrift-store chair and couch. Conner placed his guitar down on the sofa, then ambled over to the mirror, taking in his reflection.

He was surprised to see how red the whites of his eyes looked. Sure, he'd had some vodka, but he didn't expect to look like *this*—kind of worn out and tired. Conner stepped closer to the mirror, taking a closer look. His skin was ugly and pale. Maybe he'd had too much vodka? Maybe he shouldn't have had more than a sip?

Nah. Conner rolled back his shoulders, feeling loose. Relaxed. Compared to that, what was a little red-eye? There was no question that the alcohol had helped him more than it had hurt him. Conner was pumped. He was ready to play. And he was going to kick some serious butt out there.

Wasn't that all that mattered?

Jeremy Aames

<u>Cool</u> <u>Places</u> <u>to</u> <u>Take</u> <u>Jade</u>
The LA farmers' market
A Lakers game
Hyde Park for a hike
Murray's Clam Shack
And when we're ready (soon!), a
romantic dinner at L'Escale

Jade Wu

<u>Guys</u> <u>I'd</u> <u>Like</u> <u>to</u> <u>Hook</u> <u>Up</u> <u>With</u>
Conner McDermott (just once)
Angel Desmond (He and Tia broke up, all right?)
Todd Wilkins (but only on a day when he looks cute)
Christian, my next-door neighbor (age doesn't really matter)
Gavin Rossdale (You never know. . . .)

CHAPTER 9
Bad Move

Tia had no idea what she was doing here.

Well, okay, *literally* she was sitting next to Andy, at a square-shaped table on the raised-platform section of The Shack, the area behind the dancing/moshing space right in front of the stage. Obviously Tia had parked her butt in this smoky room to hear Conner play.

But what Tia was wondering as she picked up the damp napkin that the waitress had served her soda on was if she had completely lost her mind. *Conner's been such a jerk,* she thought, starting to shred the napkin in tiny pieces. *And you're still here to support him.* There was nothing left of Tia's napkin to shred, so she automatically reached for Andy's. *You should just—*

"Whoa, killer." Andy put his hand on Tia's, disrupting her inner tirade. "I think one napkin sacrifice will do."

Tia glanced down, observing the pile of paper debris in front of her. "Oh. Sorry," she said, drawing back her hand.

Andy gave her a sympathetic look. "Thinking about Angel?"

"What?" Tia's stomach turned over. What did he have to go and bring up Angel for? Thinking about *Conner* gave her enough of a heartache as it was. "No. Not until *you* mentioned him."

Andy winced. "Sorry." He sat back in his seat, hanging one arm against the back of his chair. "Think I'll just shut up now."

"Thank you." Tia sighed, stirring her soda around with her straw. She hadn't meant to snap at Andy—in fact, she felt pretty bad that she hadn't gotten a chance to talk to him again about what he'd told her on Sunday. But this definitely wasn't the time and place for it, and besides—Andy had said that he wasn't ready to get into it, so she didn't want to push him. No one else had brought up Andy's revelation this week either. Maybe they all just assumed the same thing—that Andy would say more when he wanted to.

"Hey, guys!"

Tia turned around to see that Elizabeth had arrived, with Jessica following a few steps behind. Elizabeth, obviously dressed up for the occasion in a short, black skirt and a gray wraparound shirt with a plunging neckline, looked like she might burst from happiness. Her eyes were dancing, her cheeks were slightly flushed, and now she stood above Tia, grasping onto her shoulders with palpable excitement.

Tia and Andy both said their hellos to the Wakefield sisters. Jessica, clearly in a completely opposite mood from her twin, dropped down across

127

from Andy with a heavy sigh. Meanwhile Elizabeth was still clinging to Tia's shoulders.

"I'm gonna go backstage and wish Conner luck," Elizabeth told Tia, pulling off her jacket and hanging it on the back of one of the seats as Jessica and Andy began to chat. She fixed her hair, pushing it away from her face. "You should come."

Yeah. Great idea. Tia loved Elizabeth and everything, but the girl just did not seem to get it. "I don't think so." Tia shook her head. "Conner doesn't want to see me. But you go ahead." Tia turned back around, facing the table. She lifted her glass of Coke and sipped it.

Elizabeth pulled out the chair that was next to Tia, plopping down into it. "Tee, no offense, but I think your little argument is silly."

Tia nearly spit up her soda. She placed the glass back down on the table. "What?"

Elizabeth touched Tia's arm. "Don't be mad, but Conner told me what your fight was about."

Tia blinked. He *what?* He *told* her? Wait a second. There was no possible way that Conner had told Elizabeth everything. If he had, Elizabeth most definitely would not be chatting away with Tia as if she didn't have a care in the world.... *Right?*

The back of Tia's neck began to sweat. She reached around, lifting up her dark hair to cool off. "He did? I mean ... what did he tell you?"

Elizabeth leaned forward, her light eyes opening

wide. "Just that you were upset that no one called you for Reese's birthday."

Tia stared back at Elizabeth blankly as frustration started to wash over her. She couldn't believe it. Conner had made up a blatant lie for Elizabeth. One that made Tia look petty and stupid on top of it.

"Don't get me wrong," Elizabeth went on. "I understand why you were hurt. But it's not worth staying mad at him, is it? Especially on his big night?"

Suddenly Tia felt energized. It was amazing what a little fresh anger could do. "Yeah. You're right," she said, standing up and clenching her teeth. "Let's go backstage. I'll wish Conner luck."

A smile broke out on Elizabeth's face. "Great." She stood as well, immediately heading for the back. Tia followed slowly.

Whatever. She'd wish Conner luck. But there were a couple of other things she wanted to do while she was at it. Like make him tell the truth.

And kill him if I have the chance.

Jessica really did *not* want to watch Jade and Jeremy snuggle together at a little round table at The Shack. Nor did she want to observe them laughing, obviously over something Jade had just said. And she *really* did not want to see Jeremy plant a tender kiss on Jade's cheek.

But since Jade and Jeremy were sitting diagonally across from Jessica—Jeremy with his back to her and

129

Jade facing her—Jessica had the pleasure of witnessing all of these intimate events and more. Jessica crumpled up the white paper napkin she was holding in her hands, her heart constricting as she continued to watch the two of them. Watched how Jeremy leaned across the table to take Jade's hand in his. Watched how Jade reached up and ruffled Jeremy's thick, black hair. Jessica tried to swallow back the lump that was beginning to form in her throat. It was so unfair! Jade was callously seeing someone behind Jeremy's back, but meanwhile Jeremy was mad at *Jessica*.

Jessica was so angry, she could scream. And she was so hurt, she could cry. Besides, what were they doing here anyway? Jeremy wasn't even friends with Conner. *Wait.* Was it Jessica's imagination, or was Jade shooting her a triumphant look? *Ugh.* Jade had probably brought him to the show just so she could gloat. Jessica narrowed her eyes at Jade, silently cursing her. *The little—*

"Jealous much, Jess?"

Startled, Jessica turned to look at the person who had addressed her. Andy was tilting his red-haired head in Jade and Jeremy's direction.

Jessica's mouth fell open. She threw the crumpled-up napkin at Andy's head. "I am *not* jealous."

"Man. What is it with you girls and napkins?" Andy complained, ducking as the wadded-up ball missed his head.

"Come on," Maria argued. She and Ken had arrived a little while ago and were sitting next to

130

Andy. "If you're not even the least bit jealous, then why have you been staring at them for the past five minutes?"

"Because." Jessica sighed. She stared down at the wooden table, where someone had carved R. K. + B. W. with a knife. She traced the grooves of the *B* with her finger, frustrated that she had to explain herself. Especially when *Jade* was the one who needed to do some serious explaining. "Whatever. Maybe I am a little jealous. But that's not what this is about."

Maria raised an eyebrow and smirked. "Uh-huh."

"Really!" Jessica gripped onto the edge of the table. Now her head started to pound. She shot another glance in Jade and Jeremy's direction, and her stomach turned over. "Look, Jade's cheating on Jeremy, all right?" she hissed through her teeth.

For a moment Andy, Maria, and Ken all simply stared back at Jessica with wide eyes. Jessica sat back in her chair, crossing her arms over her chest as she took in her friends' surprised reactions. *There.* Maybe now they would leave her alone.

"Really?" Maria asked finally, glancing over her shoulder to look at the couple in question.

Jessica nodded. "Yes. She even admitted it to me." At least everyone would now realize that Jade was the bad girl, not Jessica.

"That sucks," Ken said, watching Jade and Jeremy as well.

"Okay. I got a question." Andy scratched his

head, lifting his glass of ginger ale. "What does this have to do with you?"

Jessica sat up straight, moving to the edge of her ripped brown leather seat cushion and staring at Andy with obvious annoyance. "Jeremy is my friend. I don't want him to get hurt," she explained. Shouldn't all this be perfectly obvious?

"Yeah, but there's not really anything you can do about it," Ken put in, running a hand through his blond hair.

"Of course there is!" Maria exclaimed. She reached across the table to touch Jessica's arm, her bracelets jangling. "You have to tell him. You can't let this go on."

"I *did* tell him," Jessica complained, letting out a shaky sigh. She knew she was whining, but she didn't care. "He totally lost it on me."

Andy sucked in air through his teeth, looking pained. "Ooh. Bad move, Jess."

Jessica slumped against the straight wooden back of her chair, feeling more miserable by the second. "Thanks a lot," she mumbled, rolling her eyes.

"Uh, yeah, that's sorta what I was saying," Ken added. "If Jeremy's into Jade, he's not gonna want to hear anything bad about her."

"What?" Maria's dark eyebrows shot up to the ceiling. "Are you serious? Even if it's true?"

Ken shrugged. "Yeah. It's just one of those things, I guess. He has to find out for himself."

Maria shook her head in disbelief, her short, dark curls flying around her face. "Well. That's just completely idiotic."

Jessica took another painful glance at Jeremy and Jade as they talked and laughed and cuddled some more.

She had to agree. Ken's statement *was* completely idiotic. But she also knew from firsthand experience that he was right. She couldn't try to tell Jeremy anything else about Jade. He would only hate Jessica more.

Jessica shut her eyes, beyond depressed. Unfortunately, the idiot was just going to have to discover everything for himself.

Tia had run through so many painful punishment possibilities for Conner in the couple of minutes that it had taken her and Elizabeth to locate him in the back room of The Shack that she hadn't even stopped to consider what she would do if she was faced with the most likely scenario.

What if Conner was drunk?

Well, she should have thought about that. Because the minute Tia glimpsed Conner sitting hunched over on that ancient yellow-and-green plaid couch, staring at his guitar on the floor and looking all pale and clammy, she knew that he was more than slightly buzzed.

Oh, perfect, Conner, Tia thought, her stomach sinking. *Get trashed for your big performance.*

"Hey, there!" Elizabeth called to him in a cheery voice.

Tia glanced at her friend. Obviously she was still clueless.

Conner looked up. Even from where Tia was standing, she could see the rims of red surrounding Conner's green eyes. "Hey," he said in a tone that was way too mellow, especially for him. He stood, jutting his chin in their direction. "What're you guys doing back here?"

"We came to wish you luck," Elizabeth explained, watching Conner carefully. She stepped closer to him, and worry creases popped up across her forehead. "Conner?" she asked. "Are you feeling all right?"

Tia knew she should keep her mouth shut. She honestly did. It was just that keeping her thoughts to herself was physically impossible. "Yeah. You look kinda drunk," she added.

Conner glared at her. "I'm *fine*." He glanced back at Elizabeth. "So. What's up?"

"Not much," Elizabeth told him. She bit her lip, pushing a strand of hair behind her ear. Tia had known Elizabeth long enough to realize that these were her nervous gestures. Clearly she was now concerned. And Tia was glad. Well . . . as glad as she could be, given the circumstances. She was just relieved that Elizabeth was finally waking up and smelling the coffee.

Elizabeth linked her finger through one of Conner's jeans' belt loops. "Sweetie, have you been drinking?"

Conner rolled his eyes. "No," he snapped. He pushed

away from Elizabeth, stepping backward. But as he did, he stumbled, somehow tripping over his own foot.

Lovely. "You're telling us you haven't had *anything* to drink tonight?" Tia demanded, placing a hand on her hip.

Conner's jaw visibly tensed. "Actually, *Mom*, I had a little vodka, if it's all right with you," he told her, his eyes flashing with anger. He shook his head, letting out a short breath. "And I'm fine." He stormed toward the minifridge in the corner of the room, tripping over himself a second time.

Elizabeth shot Tia a worried glance as Conner reached into the fridge and pulled out a small bottle of water. But Tia was at a loss. She'd seen Conner in this condition before. And as far as she could tell, there was nothing they could do about it.

Elizabeth slowly walked toward Conner as he gulped down some water. She was twirling her silver necklace around her finger—another signature nervous-Elizabeth move. "Conner, maybe you shouldn't go out there tonight. I mean, not like this."

Conner pulled the bottle out of his mouth and threw it across the room. Drops of water flew everywhere as the plastic vessel bounced across the scratched wooden floor. Elizabeth and Tia both flinched.

"Thanks for your support!" he snapped, right in Elizabeth's face. His words came out slightly slurred.

Elizabeth grasped onto his arm, visibly scared. "Conner, I—"

"No!" he interrupted, flinging away her hand. "Get the hell off me."

Great. Tia swallowed. Conner had totally lost it. He was a mess. "Conner, Liz is right," Tia stated, trying to remain as calm as possible. "You shouldn't play. Not in this condition."

Conner kicked at the plastic water bottle, making a loud, crunching sound. "Yeah? Well, you two should get the hell out." He glared at Tia, then at Elizabeth. Elizabeth's eyes welled with tears. "I'm going out there."

Tia noticed a single tear make its way down Elizabeth's cheek.

"Just get out!" Conner yelled again.

Without saying another word, Elizabeth turned and walked out the flimsy wooden door. Tia gave Conner one last look, then followed her friend out of the room, feeling like all of her energy had been sapped away.

The ironic thing was, Tia had wanted Elizabeth to know what was going on with Conner. But now she couldn't help thinking that she wished Elizabeth hadn't had to see it.

Actually, Tia wished *she* hadn't seen Conner behave that way.

Elizabeth glanced at Tia over her shoulder. Elizabeth's eyes were all watery, and her complexion was blotchy and flushed.

Tia's stomach sank to the floor.

And now all of Sweet Valley was going to witness Conner's drunk routine.

Lila Fowler

To: foxy@swiftnet.com
From: lila3@cal.rr.com
Subject: Jade

  Tell me this. Tell me why Jade
thinks she has any right to go after
Josh. And what could Josh possibly see
in her?
  I need to know. Even though I am
totally over him anyway.

Melissa Fox

To: lila3@cal.rr.com
From: foxy@swiftnet.com
Subject: re: Jade

Lila:

Trust me. Josh is <u>really</u> not worth getting upset about. He's cute and everything, but he's not boyfriend material, as you know. And Jade's a slut. Josh'll hook up with her and move on.

But I agree with you—she has some nerve. She just better keep her claws away from Will. Not that she'd have a chance with him anyway.

Talk to you later.

Liss

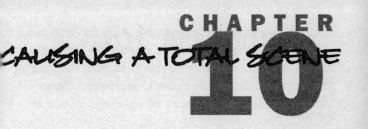
It was only eight-thirty, and already it had been a really long night.

Tia sighed as she glanced down at Elizabeth's watch. Conner was going to be onstage any minute. Part of Tia just wanted to go home. She couldn't bear the thought of seeing her best friend embarrass himself in front of this entire, packed club. But then again, despite everything, she wanted to be here for Conner if he needed her. And chances were, he would.

Tia sat back in her wooden chair, pulling her long, dark hair up into a messy bun as her friends continued to joke around and laugh. She and Elizabeth hadn't said much to each other in the fifteen minutes since the Conner incident backstage.

"Hey. You guys okay?" Maria asked, placing her dark, slender elbows on the old wooden table. She leaned forward, resting her chin in her hands and taking Tia and Elizabeth in with her deep brown eyes. "You've both been so quiet."

"Oh . . . yeah." Elizabeth sat up from her slumped position and forced a smile. "We're just tired. Right,

139

Tee?" She turned her head, glancing at Tia for backup.

"Mmmm. Yeah. Right," Tia responded, although she didn't know why they were bothering to hide the problem from Maria. In a couple of minutes the entire room was going to know why she and Elizabeth were so preoccupied.

At that moment a thirtyish-looking guy with disheveled curly hair, large wire-frame glasses, and a T-shirt hugging his potbelly walked out onto the stage and took the microphone in his hand. "Good evening, folks!" he called out. "Welcome to The Shack."

A girl a couple of tables away from Tia whistled.

"Thank you." The man onstage laughed. He shaded his eyes with his hand, scanning the crowd. "I'll come find you after the show."

Most people in the audience chuckled, but Tia completely missed the joke. She glanced over at Elizabeth, who wasn't laughing either. Her eyes were trained on the stage, her mouth a thin, straight line.

"Anyway," the man said, "we've got a great show for you tonight, kicking off with a Shack newcomer." Elizabeth grasped onto Tia's hand. Tia swallowed.

"Yeah, McD!" yelled out Evan, who was sitting a couple of tables away with the whole El Carro crew.

"I see some of his fans are here," the man commented. Everyone at Tia and Elizabeth's table cheered and screamed in response—except Tia and Elizabeth.

"All right, all right, let's just bring him out here. I give you Conner McDermott!"

Now the crowd—especially Tia's table—roared. Tia's head pounded and her heart raced as the man jumped off the stage. And then, ever so slowly, Conner ambled out from backstage with his guitar, squinting from the intensity of the bright lights.

Tia cringed, forgetting that she'd been angry and feeling only sympathy for him. *Please don't trip, please don't trip*, she thought, squeezing Elizabeth's hand.

"Go, Conner!" Andy screamed out.

Conner glanced out into the crowd and nodded in response. More screams and cheers. Then Conner walked over to the wooden stool behind the microphone in the middle of the stage—*without tripping*—and sat down. "Thanks," he said gruffly as he pulled his guitar up onto his lap.

A couple of people from the crowd whistled. Conner ducked his head and mumbled "thanks" again. Tia scrunched her eyes shut. Oh God, she couldn't watch this. She really couldn't watch this. Why was she even still here?

"This one's a new one," she heard Conner say.

Great, Tia thought, chewing on the inside of her lip. *Try out new material when you're wasted*.

"Called 'Release,'" he added.

Tia's heart was now pounding against her rib cage. *Just play*, she thought. She needed to get this over with already.

As if he'd heard Tia, Conner began to strum out the first few chords. *"Just don't tell me you know*

141

when you don't," he slowly began to sing. Elizabeth's grip on Tia's hand loosened. *"And never say you will when you won't."*

Tia slowly opened her eyes. *Whoa.* Conner actually sounded okay. No, more than okay. And he was holding his balance up there onstage. He looked together. With it.

"Release me . . ."

He sounded *incredible.* Better than he had when he'd played at HOJ. Was Tia imagining this? She turned her head, scanning the crowd. People in the audience were already cheering and yelling.

". . . Release me . . ."

Maria swiveled around in her chair to glance at Elizabeth. Her dark eyes were dancing with excitement. "He's awesome, Liz!" Maria exclaimed, then quickly turned back around to watch Conner again.

Tia and Elizabeth glanced at each other. Tia could tell that her friend was as dumbfounded as she was. And there seemed to be only one possible explanation for Conner's stellar performance. But it didn't make sense. At least, not to Tia.

She looked back at the stage and watched as Conner expertly strummed his guitar, his voice completely on key.

Could she and Elizabeth have been wrong?

Jessica was trying to figure out a way to cut out early and go home.

Okay, yeah, she knew she should've been focusing all of her energy on Conner and everything since he was still playing up on the stage. And he *was* her sister's boyfriend. Not to mention that even in Jessica's fogged-out state, she could tell that he was actually very good.

But it was no use. Jessica's brain was too crammed with thoughts of Jade and Jeremy for her to concentrate on anything else. She had switched her seat so that at least she didn't have to watch the lovebirds cozying up to each other anymore, but just knowing that they were in the same room as her made it impossible for Jessica to sit still. It took all of the restraint she had not to just march over there and make Jade tell Jeremy the truth.

No. You have to stay out of it, Jessica reminded herself, tapping her pale pink fingernails against the table. If Jessica tried to clue Jeremy in again, he would hate her forever. Or at least until he caught Jade in the act. *Which might never happen.*

Groaning, Jessica stood up, deciding to go over to the bar and get a Sprite. Maybe the simple activity would help to distract her a bit. Take her mind off things. Jessica straightened out her fitted tank sweater and headed in the bar's direction.

Unfortunately, walking to the other side of the club only raised the level of Jessica's annoyance. The Shack was now pretty crowded, and Jessica had to weave her way around chairs and bopping bodies, tripping over people's legs every couple of seconds. The room was also very hot and stuffy, filled with smoky, beer-infused air, and Jessica felt beads of perspiration beginning to form at her hairline.

Now Jessica *needed* that soda. She was looking forward to taking a cold, ice-cube-filled glass and holding it against her flushed cheeks. Of course, when she finally reached the bar area that was to the left of the stage, it was totally packed. Jessica sighed. Nothing was going to go her way tonight, was it?

She was just about to gather her energy to push her way up to the bartender's line of vision when she noticed Jade strolling out of the bathroom that was in the little alcove just off the bar. Jessica's nostrils actually *flared*. Was Jade's mission in life to torture Jessica?

Ignore her. Don't even look at her, Jessica told herself. And she intended to do just that. She truly did. But then she saw Josh Radinsky walking from the other direction toward the bathrooms. A cocky, lopsided smile appeared on his face when he zeroed in on Jade.

Jessica froze in place as she watched Josh proceed to greet Jade and corner her against the wall. Then Jessica didn't even stop to think what she was doing. She simply ran over to the wall that was perpendicular to the one Jade and Josh were leaning against and listened. Hey. Cheating was a bigger crime than eavesdropping, wasn't it? Luckily the guilty pair were standing right around the corner, and Jessica could hear every word they said.

"I like that skirt," Josh told Jade. Jessica rolled her eyes. Of course he did. The bright orange material barely covered Jade's butt.

"I made it myself," Jade informed him.

"Really? Cool. Would you make me something one day?"

Again Jessica rolled her eyes. *This* was what Jade was cheating on Jeremy for? How lame.

"Maybe," Jade said, an obvious flirtatious tone to her voice. "If you're good."

"Oh, I'll try to be," Josh said.

Oh, please. Jessica could really hurl on the spot from all the cheese that was flying between these two. She was almost ready to just walk away and get her Sprite when Josh's next words stopped Jessica in her tracks.

"A bunch of us are going to Crescent Beach after the show." His voice had deepened, and there was a very suggestive tone to it. "Whaddya say you ditch the loser you're with and come along?"

Jessica clenched her mouth shut as a surge of anger passed over her. How dare he call Jeremy a loser! *Josh* was the one who needed some serious—

"Sounds fun," Jade responded simply, disrupting Jessica's inner rantings. "I'll meet you there."

What? Jessica's eyes nearly popped out of her skull. Okay, this was really way too much. Jade wasn't only hurting Jeremy; she was completely humiliating him. Jessica's stomach turned as she thought about how Jade hadn't even bothered to defend Jeremy.

Jessica stalked away, not wanting to hear another word. She didn't have to. She already knew that Jade was treating Jeremy in a beyond-horrible way.

Once again Jessica navigated her way around the club, heading for the front doors so that she could get the fresh air she now desperately needed. And by the time she made it outside, Jessica had made an important decision.

Forget what Ken had told her. Forget what she had told herself.

Jeremy needed to know what was going on. And Jessica was going to make sure he found out. Period.

Tia kicked at the gravel in the parking lot of The Shack, still completely baffled. How had Conner managed to sober up so quickly? How had he played so perfectly when just minutes before Tia had seen him completely lose it?

"I shouldn't have said anything to him," Elizabeth mumbled quietly to Tia.

The rest of their friends—Andy, Ken, Maria, Jessica, and Evan, plus a crew of the El Carro guys—were all standing outside as well, excitedly buzzing and laughing about Conner's performance. But Tia and Elizabeth were standing off to the side a bit by themselves, both trying to figure out exactly what had happened with Conner tonight.

Tia buttoned up her jean jacket. "Liz, you had to say something. He was acting nuts."

Elizabeth cast her eyes down to her strappy black sandals. "Yeah . . . maybe . . . but—"

"Hey! Is that *the* Conner McDermott?" Andy suddenly called out.

Tia and Elizabeth both glanced toward The Shack. Conner was strolling out through a swinging door in the back, his guitar case slung across his chest. He shed a small smile as he approached the group, and everyone started to clap and cheer.

"You were incredible!" Maria called out as he came closer.

Evan walked over and slapped Conner on the back. "Killer show, man."

"Thanks," Conner responded as more friends went on to express their praise. But then, seemingly all of a sudden, his face turned strangely serious, with his jaw set in a tight line.

At first Tia thought Conner was embarrassed from all the attention. But then Conner looked right at her, and she caught the angry glint in his eye.

Uh-oh, she thought, chewing on the inside of her lip. *He's pissed. At me.*

Conner stalked toward Tia and Elizabeth, not even bothering to recognize any of the other compliments that people were rushing over to give him. Tia didn't need to look at Elizabeth to see how she was reacting.

She could feel the anxiety vibes shooting out of Elizabeth's body.

Whatever, Tia thought. *We didn't do anything wrong. In fact, he owes us an apology.*

"Conner, you were—," Elizabeth quickly began as he neared them.

"Happy now?" Conner demanded, cutting her off. He glared at Elizabeth, then at Tia. "See? I told you I'd be fine."

Great. He was yelling. And now everyone was staring. It was one thing if he wanted to be mad at Tia and Elizabeth (even though he didn't really have a right to be), but there was no reason to cause a total scene.

"Conner," Tia started, stuffing her hands into her jacket pockets. "Don't even—"

"Shut up," Conner interrupted. He pointed his finger right in Tia's face. "I don't want to hear it from you!" He moved his finger and pointed it at Elizabeth. "Or you. And don't ever tell me when and where I can drink again! And *never* tell me when and where I can play!"

Tia swallowed as her face began to heat up. She had never seen Conner act like this. Ever. She was about to say something to argue back, then thought better of it. Obviously there was no reasoning with Conner tonight. She glanced at Elizabeth. Her eyes had filled up with tears as Conner continued to glare at her.

Everyone in the parking lot was completely silent, looking shell-shocked from Conner's outburst.

Tia felt nauseous and shaky, and everyone's faces started to blur together. Finally Conner tore his fierce gaze off Elizabeth and turned to look at Evan and the other El Carro guys.

"Come on," he said, his voice much quieter now. He ambled over to them. "Time to party."

Evan ran a hand through his longish black hair. "Uh, buddy?" he began, obviously uncomfortable. "Maybe we should all just go home."

Thank you, Evan, Tia thought, letting out a heavy breath.

But Conner wouldn't have it. He shook his head, his shoulders visibly stiffening. "*I'm* going to Crescent Beach. Either you're in or you're out," he snapped, then stalked off toward his Mustang.

Evan momentarily closed his eyes, looking defeated.

"What was *that?*" Andy asked.

"You guys, he can't get behind the wheel," Maria pointed out.

Tia couldn't agree more. But she felt hopeless. She didn't know how to stop Conner. It was like a monster had taken over his body.

Evan looked at Tia and Elizabeth. "Listen, I'll take care of this, all right?"

Elizabeth just nodded, still looking stunned.

"Yeah. Thanks, Evan," Tia responded softly.

"No problem," Evan said. He turned to Reese, Tommy, and Scott. "Come on, guys. Let's go." And then all four guys took off, jogging to catch Conner before he got into his car.

Tia hugged herself as she watched Evan run up to Conner and slide into the driver's seat of Conner's Mustang. At least Conner wasn't putting up a fight about driving—maybe somewhere inside he realized what a bad idea that would be. Tia did feel slightly better knowing that Evan was going to watch over Conner. But only slightly. And it didn't erase that unsettling feeling that was forming in the pit of her stomach.

The feeling that something horrible was going to happen.

Conner McDermott

People are overrated.

They disappoint you. They get on your case. They nag. They break promises. They always want something in return. And they take away your freedom.

So, yeah. Love's all right. But I'm starting to think that being alone is better.

CHAPTER 11
Ignoring the Guilt

Whoa. Now *that* was scary.

Jessica's heart twisted as she saw the look of total despair on her sister's face. Jessica had no idea what had really happened, but part of her wanted to go run after Conner and kick his butt for yelling at Elizabeth that way. Regardless of what she had done, Jessica knew that her twin didn't deserve to be treated like that. And it was also painfully clear that Conner's outburst had been alcohol induced.

Between this disaster and the whole Jade-Jeremy situation, this evening had turned into one of the most miserable nights in the Wakefield sisters' history.

Sighing, Jessica wandered over to Elizabeth. Maria was standing next to her, her arm slung across Elizabeth's shoulders. "Hey, are you all right?" Jessica asked, brushing a strand of Elizabeth's blond hair away from her eyes.

Elizabeth nodded, kicking at the ground. "Yeah. I think so," she mumbled.

Maria dropped her arm from Elizabeth's shoulders.

"Why was he so worked up anyway? What was that about?"

Elizabeth glanced up, fidgeting with a loose thread that was hanging off the bottom of her jacket. "Do you mind if we don't talk about this? I think I just want to go home and go to bed."

Maria nodded sympathetically. "Are you sure?"

"Yes," Elizabeth responded. "I'm just too drained to think right now."

"Fine. I'll call you tomorrow, all right?"

Elizabeth let out a shaky breath. "Yeah."

Maria kissed Elizabeth's cheek, then turned and hooked her arm through Ken's, leading him over to his car. "Call me later if you need anything!" Maria added over her shoulder.

Jessica bit her lip and shifted her weight from one foot to the other, wondering what to do next. She really, really wanted to be there for her sister. The problem was, if Jessica was going to take care of this whole Jade issue, she was going to have to move fast. And if Elizabeth truly *was* just going to go to sleep . . .

"Liz? Are you sure that you don't want to talk about this tonight?" Jessica asked. She stuck the zipper of her black cotton jacket in her mouth and chewed on it as she waited for a response.

Elizabeth held a hand up to her temples, wincing from apparent pain. "Yes. Why?"

Jessica dropped the zipper. "Well, it's just that I'm totally here if you need me. *Totally*. But if not, there's

153

something I need to take care of, like, now."

"Go ahead." Elizabeth dropped her hands. "I'll be fine." She glanced over at Andy and Tia, who were quietly talking by Andy's car. "Andy? Can you give me a ride home?" she called.

Andy nodded. "'Course. No problem."

Elizabeth turned back to Jessica, digging into her jacket pockets and pulling out the car keys. "So go. Take the Jeep."

"Thanks," Jessica responded, taking the keys in her hand and trying to ignore the guilt that was threatening to overcome her. Jessica hesitated for a moment, searching her sister's face. "You're sure?"

"Yes," Elizabeth insisted. "Now go already."

Jessica smiled. Elizabeth was practically forcing her to go. There was no reason to feel the least bit guilty. "Okay. I love you." She hugged Elizabeth tightly. "Feel better. And we'll talk tomorrow."

"All right." Elizabeth sighed, pulling away.

And with that, Jessica ran off, car keys in hand, ready to attack problem number one.

Jessica took one final glance at her sister before climbing into the Jeep. The girl did not look good.

Tomorrow Jessica would definitely deal with problem number two.

Jeremy was very glad that he hadn't listened to Jessica.

Because if he had, he wouldn't be standing with

Jade in front of her door right now, staring into her gorgeous, lively, almond-shaped eyes or holding her soft hands. Nor would he have been able to admire her shapely legs in that short skirt she was wearing. But most of all, he wouldn't have had the amazing night that he'd just experienced. A night that proved to him that Jade was definitely not seeing anybody else. And that she was completely, without a question, one hundred percent into him.

"I'm sorry I had to cut our date short." Jade reached up and ran her fingers through Jeremy's wavy hair. His spine tingled from her touch. "But I have to be up early in the morning."

"I understand." Jeremy grinned, squeezing her hands. "That must be hard for you, considering you usually sleep until two."

Jade's dark eyes widened. "Right. True."

She had a funny, unreadable expression on her face. Was it surprise? Or annoyance? Jeremy swallowed. *Did I screw up?* he wondered nervously. Maybe Jade was insulted by his observation of her late-sleeping habits?

But then suddenly, without any sort of warning, she reached up and kissed him.

Guess she's not mad. Jeremy kissed Jade back, his entire body on fire from the passionate way Jade was pressing her lips to his. He ran one hand through her silky dark hair, thinking that this was much more than a kiss. This was . . . a *kiss.* Then Jade massaged the back of Jeremy's head with her fingernails, and goose bumps prickled the entire length of his neck.

Jeremy could have stood there for hours, the crisp night air encircling him as his limbs continued to heat up from Jade's tender touches. He could have stayed in that position for *days*. But of course, they had to stop at some point.

"Thanks. I had fun," Jade told him, pulling away.

Jeremy's hand lingered in her hair. "So you wanna go out again?" he asked, his heart pounding in his ears as a result of both nervousness and the kiss. "Like sometime next week?"

Jade's black eyes lit up. The corners of her mouth drew up into a smile. "Sure. Of course."

Of course? She said, "Of course"! As in "no-brainer." As in I definitely like you. A lot. "Great! I mean, cool."

Jade laughed. "I'll call you, okay?"

She'll call me? Jeremy's pulse was quickening by the second. This was, without a doubt, one of the best nights of his life. "Sure. Okay." Then he leaned down and gave Jade one last kiss. A kiss that he wished could go on forever. "Well, good night," he told her finally, breaking away.

"Good night, Jeremy." With those words, Jade turned around and unlocked her front door. She gave Jeremy a final wave, then disappeared inside her apartment.

Jeremy stood in the courtyard of the complex for a moment, absorbing everything that had happened in the past few hours. He couldn't help smiling as it dawned on him that this thing with Jade was turning into something very real. Like a relationship.

Jeremy began to stroll over to his car, realizing that he'd learned a lot about Jade tonight. For one, she was even cooler than he'd originally thought. And sexier. And funnier.

But perhaps the best thing he'd discovered was that there was no way that what Jessica had told him was true.

Jeremy unlocked his car, elated. If there was one thing he knew for sure, it was that Jade was *not* cheating on him.

So far, this car ride had been pure torture.

Ever since Tia, Elizabeth, and Andy had driven away from The Shack five minutes ago, Andy's car had been filled with a heavy, uncomfortable silence.

Tia glanced sideways at Andy. He had an uncharacteristically grim expression as he drove, his blue eyes trained on the curvy road in front of him. Normally you could count on Andy to break the tension with a few well-timed quips. But tonight he didn't seem to be in a joking mood.

Tia slumped back in her seat. *Andy's just as freaked out by Conner as the rest of us,* she realized. *And it's not like he doesn't have tons on his mind to begin with,* she told herself, feeling another twinge of guilt about how she'd let her friend down.

Tia turned around to look at Elizabeth, who was

sitting in the backseat. Elizabeth was staring out the window blankly, absently picking at the door lock. Her skin was unnaturally pale, and her mouth was drawn into a thin, tight line. Tia only hoped that she wasn't blaming herself.

"Liz," Tia began carefully, "he somehow managed to pull off that show. But he *was* drunk. He really was."

Elizabeth sighed. She didn't take her eyes off the passing dark scenery. "I know."

"So you did the right thing," Tia continued. "We did the right thing. He didn't give us a choice."

Elizabeth's gaze dropped to her hands. "I don't know," she responded quietly. "He drank because he was nervous. That's normal, right? I shouldn't have given him such a hard time."

Tia's eyes widened. Elizabeth thought that Conner's temper tantrum had been *normal*? Under whose definition? "But Liz, he doesn't only drink before shows," she argued.

"And he did seem pretty out of control," Andy put in, turning on his signal to make a left. "I mean, he—"

"You guys?" Elizabeth broke in, cutting Andy off. Finally she glanced up. Her eyes looked worn and tired. "I really can't talk about this right now, okay?"

There she went on that denial trip again. Tia glanced at Andy. He gave her a wary look, shrugging. "Yeah. Okay," he said, making his left turn. "Whatever you want."

"Thanks," Elizabeth responded quietly, then went

back to her staring-out-the-window routine.

Tia turned back around in her seat, dejected. She knew that it was toxic for Elizabeth to ignore Conner's issues the way she was. And Tia also was aware of the fact that there was no way they could help Conner if they didn't all recognize his problem.

But what could Tia do? She couldn't force Elizabeth to talk about it.

So Tia simply shut her mouth and turned on the radio. At least *that* would create some noise.

Oh, you've got to be kidding me.

This was some sort of joke, right? Jeremy had managed to ignore Jessica all night at The Shack, but now here she was, sitting on his *doorstep?* Unbelievable.

Jeremy shook his head as he locked his car, then cut across the lawn toward his front door. What was Jessica thinking? And of course, she had to look beautiful too, her blond hair shining under his house's bright exterior lights.

Not that it mattered. Jeremy was still completely mad at her, gorgeous or not.

Jessica quickly stood as he approached, rubbing her palms against the sides of her tight-fitting black pants. "Jeremy."

Jeremy barely made eye contact, stopping in front of her. "What do you want, Jess?"

"Okay." Jessica bit her lip. She stepped backward so that she was standing on the brick front step, making her basically the same height as Jeremy. "I know that you don't want to hear this, but I can't help it. You've gotta come with me. I can prove that Jade's cheating on you."

"I've gotta *what*?" Was Jessica for real? Did she *ever* give up? Or was lying just a favorite hobby of hers? Jeremy began to walk past Jessica up the steps. "I don't have time for this." He fished around his khaki pants' pocket, searching for his keys. "Just go home. Enough already." Jeremy's fingers wrapped around his rubber-football key chain. He lifted his hand to unlock the door, but Jessica stopped him, grabbing onto his arm.

"No," she said firmly.

Jeremy turned to look at Jessica. Her aqua eyes were steady. Determined. Intense. "Stop playing games, Jess. Just let me go to bed."

"I am *not* playing any games," Jessica insisted. "Look, I know you think I'm only doing this because I'm jealous, and I can understand that. Sort of." Jessica's cheeks reddened at her almost admission. "But this really isn't about that. I promise. I'm only here because I care about you," she insisted, her voice soft and pleading.

Jeremy felt himself begin to soften. He still thought she was nuts, but it was also clear that she was hurting.

"So, will you come with me? Please?" Jessica dropped her hand from his arm. "Just this once and I'll leave you alone. I swear."

Jeremy sighed. This was ridiculous, but if it would get her off his back . . .

"Just this once?" he repeated, staring into her eyes.

Jessica let out a little breath. "Cross my heart and hope to die."

The girl looked like her life depended on it. Jeremy was certain she was wrong, so he figured he might as well humor her. "All right," he responded finally.

Jessica's eyes lit up. She reached up and gave Jeremy a quick hug. "Good. Let's go." She turned and began to run down the steps.

Jeremy watched her head toward her Jeep, and one thought kept repeating itself in his brain.

Why *am I doing this?*

Elizabeth Wakefield

God. Conner was so mad. And he has every right to be. I mean, I acted like I was just waiting for him to fail. Waiting for something to go wrong.

The horrible thing is, even as I lie here in bed and tell myself I was wrong—tell myself that Conner <u>can</u> handle himself tonight—deep down, I don't believe it.

And I <u>am</u> still waiting for something to go wrong.

This was definitely Jade's night.

It almost didn't seem possible. Just an hour ago Jade was at The Shack with Jeremy, having a blast as they laughed and joked and watched Conner play, generally acting the part of the cute couple.

And now here Jade was, sitting at a bonfire on Crescent Beach in between Josh's legs, his strong arms wrapped around her, his breath hitting the back of Jade's neck and shooting tingles up and down her spine. Jade squinted, staring into the burning embers of the fire. Two incredible dates with two incredible guys. Everything was going so impossibly smoothly.

Then Jade looked around at the surrounding crew and groaned inwardly. *Well, not that there couldn't be a slight improvement.* Jade knew that this was supposed to be a party and everything, but she didn't drive all the way out here—by herself—to hang out with Jake Collins. And she certainly hadn't come here to listen to Gina Cho gossip incessantly. Unfortunately, that was exactly what Jade was being forced to do at the moment.

"You should have *seen* the look on her face," Gina was telling the crowd of people huddled around the fire. "It was too much."

You're *too much*, Jade thought, rolling her eyes as she kicked away a Coke can.

Then Josh swept Jade's thick hair off her neck, making a clearing so that he could whisper right into her ear. Once again shivers traveled from the top of Jade's head down to the bottom of her back. "You wanna take a walk?" he asked gruffly.

Jade smiled. It was about time. "Yes," she told him, turning around. "Definitely."

Josh's high, chiseled cheekbones formed sharp points as he grinned. "Let's go, then." He stood, holding out a hand to help Jade up. She took it and pulled herself up from the sand.

Josh draped an arm across Jade's shoulders, and the two of them began to walk away from the group. Now things were turning around—this was exactly what Jade wanted.

"Hey, Radinsky!" Ted Masters called after them. Josh glanced over his shoulder, looking back at his friend. "Have *fun*," Ted teased. His obvious insinuation caused a few people in the group to laugh.

Jade felt her face heat up, and Josh shook his head, muttering "idiot" under his breath. He gave Jade's shoulders a squeeze. "Sorry about that."

"It's not a big deal," Jade said. And she meant it. She knew what guys like Ted thought—that Josh was pulling one over on her, that he was *scoring*. But that was so not the case. Hooking up with Josh was Jade's *choice*. And she didn't want, or expect, anything in return. Jade certainly wasn't dumb enough—unlike Lila—to think that just because she and Josh had fooled around, she was now going to have a relationship with the guy. Josh was the kind of guy you just had fun with.

"Wanna go over there?" Josh asked, pointing his flashlight at a cozy cove not that far off.

Jade eyed the spot and nodded approvingly. "Perfect." *And it really is,* she thought as they started to walk toward the area. Off to Jade and Josh's right the waves were methodically crashing against the shore, the palm trees were ruffling in the wind over to the left, soft grains of cool sand tickled Jade's bare feet, and a dark sky filled with infinite stars greeted her from above. The setting *was* absolutely perfect.

Jade loved the beach at night. It was so sensual. And romantic. And magical. The possibilities of what could happen here seemed endless.

And then, just as Josh and Jade were about to sink down onto the sand, one possibility that hadn't even entered into Jade's mind suddenly became a stark reality.

"Nice. I *thought* you were going to bed."

Jade's entire body stiffened as an uneasy feeling of dread washed over her. Josh dropped his arm from her shoulders. *It can't be him,* Jade thought—or rather hoped. But there was no mistaking the voice.

Jade slowly turned around, her stomach plummeting to her toes as she realized that at the present, she had no viable options. No lie was going to get Jade out of this one. She'd been caught.

And now Jeremy was staring her in the face.

Jessica couldn't exactly say she was happy. But she *was* relieved.

Even so, her heart broke for Jeremy as she observed the bitter disappointment in his dark brown eyes. *At least he finally knows the truth,* Jessica told herself, clutching onto her tiny purse as she watched Jeremy explode at Jade.

"Do you always blatantly lie to people? Or am I just a special case?" Jeremy asked a clearly shocked Jade. Josh had been standing right next to Jade, but as the bonfire crowd slowly crept over to see what was going on, Josh had taken a step or two back, distancing himself from the scene and uncomfortably stuffing his hands in the front pockets of his faded jeans.

Jade's eyes darted around, noticing all of the gathering faces. Even in the dark Jessica could see Jade's cheeks flame up. "Jeremy," Jade hissed, closing her thin windbreaker close to her body and hugging herself. "We never said we wouldn't see other people."

Jeremy looked up at the midnight blue sky and shook his head. "You're right. Stupid me. I assumed that was understood." He stared at Jade for a moment, as if he was trying to figure her out. Which he probably was. "So why did you lie about where you were going tonight? And what was the point of that little love note?" he asked. "Was that just to cover your tracks?"

Jessica's skin crawled as she heard Cherie Reese snicker behind her. Unfortunately, Cherie's snicker was a sound Jessica knew all too well. Her stomach now felt hollowed out and cavernous. Suddenly all she wanted to do was get Jeremy out of there. She glanced over her shoulder, taking in the amused crowd that had assembled. As much as Jessica was a full-fledged supporter of Jeremy telling Jade off, she didn't want him to cause a scene. *Jeremy hates scenes,* she thought, her stomach sinking. Not to mention that Jeremy was the stranger here—a Big Mesa guy in a Sweet Valley–El Carro crowd. *He* was going to come off as the bad guy.

Let's just go, Jessica thought, shivering from the cool night breeze. *Let's go home, and we'll talk about this.*

"Look, Jeremy, I like you and everything, but I never said anything about love," Jade argued, flipping her sleek dark hair over her shoulder. "I'm sorry if you feel more strongly than I do."

Many more snickers erupted, but Jessica's attention was focused on Jeremy. She watched as Jeremy's entire body slumped, as if he was physically stricken. Jessica felt her heart break all over again. She was torn between wanting to wring Jade's neck for her heartless comment and wanting to rush over to

Jeremy and throw her arms around him and tell him that Jade didn't deserve him. *She doesn't even deserve his left pinkie,* Jessica thought, gritting her teeth.

Then Jeremy turned to Jessica, and her eyes widened. *Come on,* she pleaded silently. *Let's go. I'll take you home.*

"What is *with* you girls?" Jeremy spat out, glancing back and forth from Jessica to Jade. "It's like lying and cheating is all you know how to do!"

Jessica gasped, feeling like the wind had been knocked out of her. Jeremy was grouping Jessica with . . . *Jade?* Jessica barely registered the loud din of laughter and people's nasty comments—she could only hear a roaring in her own ears.

How can he think of me like that? Jessica's knees felt weak and jellylike, as if they might give in at any second.

"You know what? I never want to speak to either of you again!" Jeremy snapped, then stalked off without so much as another glance in Jessica's direction.

Jessica's eyes immediately welled up with tears as Jeremy stormed toward the parking lot. A few spectators applauded and cheered, but Jessica didn't care. Her only thought was Jeremy—she wanted to chase after him and make him take back his words. But she was also too paralyzed with shock to take a step.

When Jessica *did* find the ability to move, she turned her gaze to Jade, ready to tear into her, but Jessica discovered that her mouth was paralyzed too.

Jade narrowed her eyes at Jessica, giving her an ultimate glare of hate.

Jessica didn't know how long she and Jade stood there, silently conveying their anger at each other. She was somehow aware that the crowd had begun to disperse. Then Josh loped over to Jade, rubbing the back of his neck and not meeting her eye. "Hey . . . uh, why don't we take a rain check?" he suggested, clearly uneasy from the scene that had just played out.

"Whatever," Jade muttered, still staring at Jessica.

"Okay. Cool." Josh shrugged. He slowly made his way back toward the bonfire. Leaving Jessica alone on the beach with Jade.

Which was the absolute last place on earth Jessica wanted to be.

Conner shook his head, smirking as the clusters of party goers started to head back toward the bonfire. As far as he could tell, his lame classmates had become fascinated with some soap-opera-esque event involving Jessica Wakefield.

She must be taking lessons from her sister, Conner thought, downing the remaining sips of his Budweiser. Between this scene on the beach and Elizabeth and Tia's earlier dramatics, Conner felt like he was a guest star on *Dawson's Creek.*

Well, forget Liz, he decided, smashing the aluminum can in his hand. He threw the crushed metal into the dying fire. *And forget Tia. Forget everyone.*

Conner ambled over to the six-pack-filled brown paper bag that sat next to his work boots a few feet away. He grabbed another can of Bud and popped it open. This was his night. And he was going to have fun despite the fact that everybody was getting in his face.

Conner plopped down next to the paper bag, taking a few gulps of the lukewarm beer. *Maybe if I stay away from them all, they'll leave me alone.*

"Hey, man. You ready to take off?"

Maybe not. Conner glanced up to see Evan standing before him. The guy was being such a royal pain in the butt tonight. *He probably still wants Liz's body or something. He's trying to get on her good side by acting like my baby-sitter.* Conner picked up a piece of bottle green sea grass and tossed it. "No. The party's just beginning."

Evan crouched down and sighed. "I don't mean to be a bummer, McD. But it's late. And you've had a lot to drink."

Conner lifted his eyebrows as he sipped some more beer. Was his friend for real? Since when did Evan forget how to have a good time? "You know, you're right," Conner said, pulling himself up.

Evan quickly stood as well. "Yeah? Cool."

Conner shook his head. "You *are* a bummer, man." He tossed his half-filled can down on the sand, splattering Evan with beer. "Later." Disgusted, Conner turned away, stumbling toward the outer edge of the beach. He really needed to get out of Sweet Valley.

Everyone here was so damn annoying. And uptight.

Unfortunately, right now Conner wasn't exactly in the position to move out on his own. He frowned, then stopped in place, eyeing the huge rocks and boulders that lined the beach's periphery. Well, he might be stuck here, but he *could* do his best to get away from all these freakin' people.

Now determined, Conner headed right for the rocks. He reached up, grabbing onto the cool, jagged edge of one of the boulders while he stepped onto an indentation on the steep rock with his bare foot. *There.* That was easy enough.

Conner glanced up and saw another makeshift handle to grab onto. He did so, but this time there was no place for either of his feet to rest—they slipped and dangled and kicked at the craggy rock face as his arms stretched and stretched until both arms felt like they might be pulled out of their sockets. *Damn.* Finally Conner found the tiniest bit of a groove to step on, reaching up with his hands and climbing some more.

It wasn't the easiest trip up to the highest rock, but Conner never gave up. Energized by his desire to get away from everyone else, he finally made it. Panting, he stood up straight, the wind whipping all around him. Conner felt a total rush as he looked around and realized how high up he was. Up here all alone, staring out at the endless, dark ocean, Conner felt at peace for the first time that night.

"God, man, get down! You're gonna fall!"

Conner rolled his eyes. Of course, Evan had to ruin this for him. Just like Elizabeth had ruined his gig. And just like everyone always ruined everything. Conner took a small step toward the edge and glanced down. Sure enough, Evan was standing there, staring up at him and looking like he was about to freak out.

"I'm fine. Leave me alone!" Conner yelled back.

But Evan shook his head. "I'm serious!" he called. "It's dangerous!"

Dangerous? Conner sighed. Well, maybe it was—for wimps like Evan. "Go away!" Conner stuffed his hands in his front jeans' pockets, stepping slightly forward a little more—rather close to the edge—so that Evan could see how angry he was. "Just go home, man!" And with that, Conner lifted his right foot to step back, but instead of stepping onto the rock's surface, Conner felt his toes pushing through air, through blank space.

Before he could process what was happening, Conner lost his balance, and his entire body followed in the direction of his air-bound foot. For a split second Conner was falling, and then his body crashed down to the ground.

Conner squeezed his eyes shut as he absorbed what had just happened. He'd fallen. Oddly, Conner hardly felt any pain. He hardly felt *anything*. *Thank God for sand,* he thought, wincing.

"Oh, man, Conner! You okay? You there?"

Conner slowly opened his eyes to see a blurry

Evan hovering above him. "Yeah. I'm fine." *Huh.* That had been a clean fall. No throbbing, no pain. All Conner could feel was a wetness trickling down his forehead, which he figured must be sweat.

Evan knelt down next to Conner, his eyes darting and nervous looking. "Come on. We gotta get you to a hospital." Evan swiveled around, calling over his shoulder, "Reese, get over here! Someone call 911!"

Whoa. Hospital? 911? "I told you, I'm fine," Conner insisted, rubbing his head. *Man.* How could he have sweated *that* much? Conner lifted his hand from his head and pulled it toward his eyes.

That was when he saw the blood—the bright red liquid dripping from his fingers. Seeing that, Conner's eyes rolled back into his head.

And he passed out cold.

JADE WU

11:32 P.M.

It's not like there aren't plenty of guys out there. But Jessica? The girl is dog food.

HAZEL M. LEWIS LIBRARY
POWERS, OREGON 97466

JESSICA WAKEFIELD
11:33 P.M.

Jeremy <u>didn't</u> just say that he never wanted to speak to me again. He couldn't have, right? I wasn't the one seeing someone behind his back. . . . Not this time, at least.

God. What did I do?

WILL SIMMONS
11:35 P.M.

I've got Melissa. I've got Michigan. My life is <u>set.</u>

MELISSA FOX

11:37 P.M.

Now I see that Will and I had to go through all of that stuff in the beginning of the year to be where we are now: committed to spending the rest of our lives together.

Now that we have that, nothing could possibly go wrong.

ELIZABETH WAKEFIELD

2:33 A.M.

I wish I could just fall asleep. I wish I knew where Conner was right now. If I only knew that, then I could sleep. . . .

Check out the **all-new**....

(**Sweet Valley Web site**—)

www.sweetvalley.com

New Features

Cool Prizes

The **ONLY** official Web site!

Hot Links

(And much more!)

Bantam
Bantam Doubleday Dell

BFYR 202

Francine Pascal's

SVH

senior year

You're watching
"Dawson's Creek"...

You're wearing
Urban Decay...

Have you read
senior year?

Bantam

www.sweetvalley.com

BFYR 232